IN THE SHⱥ

"The *Madame Bovary* of Turkish literature ... Although the story is, in many ways, universal, Derviş brilliantly captures the particularities of Turkish society and its struggle with modernity. This rare gem is finally available in English thanks to Maureen Freely's masterful translation."

—*The Guardian*, Top 10 Novels about Turkey

"*In the Shadow of the Yalı* is a rare gem—a romantic character study, a social novel, and a feminist critique on patriarchy and capitalism. Suat Derviş explores the depths of social conditioning, the emptiness of chasing wealth, and the freedoms—imagined or actual—provided by lust and desire."

—Ilana Masad, author of *All My Mother's Lovers*

"Evoking the tumultuous fledgling years of the Turkish Republic as it rises from the ashes of the Ottoman Empire, *In the Shadow of the Yalı* is an enthralling and troubling novel about desire, possession, and illicit love. Suat Derviş delivers a powerful feminist rebuke of patriarchal society that thrums with passion right up to the surprising and challenging climax of this romantic and tragic work."

—Alan Drew, author of *Gardens of Water*

"In this extraordinary novel, Suat Derviş gives us the awakening of Celile, a young woman who discovers both the potency of her desire and the men who want to harness that guileless joy for their own ends. Her extreme innocence allows her a full-hearted and wide-eyed view of the events she is driving by her own actions, even as they threaten to destroy her. Steamy, gothic, and deeply insightful about the tangled motivations of financial greed and romantic love, as well as the vastly divergent life options for women and men in mid-twentieth-century Turkey, I read this novel in one big gulp."

—Lucy Jane Bledsoe, author of *Lava Falls*
and *A Thin Bright Line*

"Suat Derviş is an important novelist. She suffered a great deal for her political views, and her works were suppressed ... *In the Shadow of the Yalı* is a work of beauty. A painful love story. A novel that examines love from a Marxist perspective. In my opinion, it has no equal in our literature."

—Selim İleri, Orhan Kemal Novel Prize–winning
author of *Boundless Solitude*

THE PRISONER OF ANKARA

Also by Suat Derviş

In the Shadow of the Yalı

THE
PRISONER
OF
ANKARA

SUAT DERVIŞ

Translated from the Turkish and
with an introduction by Maureen Freely

•
•
•
•
•
•
•
•

Other Press
New York

Originally published in French, translated from the Turkish, as
Le Prisonnier d'Ankara in 1957 and in Turkish as *Ankara Mahpusu* in 1968

Production editor: Yvonne E. Cárdenas
Text designer: Patrice Sheridan
This book was set in Palatino and Goudy Sans by
Alpha Design & Composition of Pittsfield, NH

1 3 5 7 9 10 8 6 4 2

Library of Congress Cataloging-in-Publication Data
Names: Derviş, Suat, author. | Freely, Maureen, 1952- translator.
Title: The prisoner of Ankara / Suat Derviş ; translated from the Turkish
and with an introduction by Maureen Freely.
Other titles: Ankara mahpusu. English
Description: New York : Other Press, 2024.
Identifiers: LCCN 2024012797 (print) | LCCN 2024012798 (ebook) |
ISBN 9781892746931 (paperback) | ISBN 9781590510285 (ebook)
Subjects: LCGFT: Novels.
Classification: LCC PL248.D4 A813 2024 (print) | LCC PL248.D4 (ebook) |
DDC 894/.3533—dc23/eng/20240731
LC record available at https://lccn.loc.gov/2024012797
LC ebook record available at https://lccn.loc.gov/2024012798

INTRODUCTION

KIMSESIZ. MOST Turkish-English dictionaries define this word as *orphan* or *outcast*. But the literal translation better captures its cultural meaning: *without anyone*. To be *kimsesiz* is to lack all manner of family and community support. As the standard Turkish dictionary definition makes clear, it is to go through life without anyone to protect you. It is also to know that when your time comes, you will have no one to take your body to the mosque to be washed, and no one to pay for your funeral. In a country that prides itself on its family and neighborhood networks, there can be no sorrier fate.

It is thanks to those networks, some say, that fewer people fall through the cracks here than elsewhere. This may be wishful thinking sustained by poor record-keeping. But to watch the speed with which Turkey's ordinary citizens respond to today's natural and political cataclysms is to know that they draw on a long tradition of compassion in action. They understand, often from their own family histories, that a *kimsesiz* (unlike an outcast) can be utterly blameless.

This cannot be said of Vasfi, the prisoner of this book's title. He is the adored and pampered son of a widow who works as a domestic to keep him in medical school—until, one night, a drunkenly misdirected crime of passion lands him behind bars. We meet him twelve years later, as he leaves behind his makeshift family of fellow inmates to walk free on the streets of Ankara. Seeing no future for himself in a city where he knows no one, he returns to his native Istanbul, but here again, he has no one, for his mother has died. It isn't long before Vasfi has gone through his meager savings and sold off any possessions of value. Soon all he has left is his pride. But as he begins his final descent into homelessness, it is his pride that almost kills him.

As the granddaughter of a pasha and the daughter of a French-trained society doctor, Suat Derviş grew up far from the mean streets she so powerfully evokes in *The Prisoner of Ankara*. It was through her work as a "journalist of the streets" during the middle to late 1930s that she first came to know them. She already had a string of Gothic novels to her name by then. She had edited the first women's page to run in a Turkish newspaper and worked as a political correspondent in France as well as Germany. She'd been allied with the left from early adulthood, but it wasn't until her father died in 1933, leaving the family in economic difficulties, that she had her own first taste of precarity. Instead of dragging her down, it gave her new questions. More than ever, she wanted to know how the poor survived.

What must an unemployed man endure before he finds work? How is a woman to make a living? What does it mean to be a child in Istanbul? Where in this city do the penniless make their homes? Who lives beneath Istanbul's streets? What happens to them after dark? These were the questions she took with her into the city's roughest neighborhoods. What she learned along the way transformed every novel she wrote thereafter.

As it did her journalism, despite the growing dangers faced by leftists in a country where thought itself could be a crime. At no point did such risks stop Derviş from speaking her mind. She was doubly notorious by now, having married the secretary-general of the Turkish Communist Party, who was serving a long prison sentence. By 1945, when *The Prisoner of Ankara* was first serialized (under its original title, *For Zeynep*), she was filing most of her journalism under pseudonyms. When even this work dwindled to the point that she could no longer support herself, she went into voluntary and almost penniless exile. It was in a small hotel in Paris that she and her sister came closest to becoming *kimsesiz*. But then the leading lights of the French

Communist Party came to their rescue. In addition to embracing them as comrades, they found Derviş a publisher. Thanks to an early governess, both she and her sister had excellent French. Together they set about translating *For Zeynep*. It was published in 1957 as *The Prisoner of Ankara*, the first novel by a Turkish woman ever to appear in France.

It was not published in book form in Turkey until 1968, when the success of her last novel, *Shimmering Çevriye*, returned her to the public eye. Derviş was back in Turkey by then, helping to found the Socialist Women's Union. But she'd been greatly weakened by her almost-*kimsesiz* years. After her death in 1972, she fell back into oblivion. It is thanks to a dedicated network of scholars that she is at last back in print to receive the credit she is due.

Like *In the Shadow of the Yalı*, the other of her novels published in French translation, *The Prisoner of Ankara* is a social-realist page-turner. It offers as many shocks and twists as an airport novel, even as it makes its politics clear. But what sets the book apart—and keeps it in my heart—is its cast of *kimsesiz* characters: the former dockworker who spends his days in the same ferry station where he lost his leg; the two ancient friends who stand by the radiator in the Grand Post Office remembering the casinos and grand liaisons that led to their ruin; the ravaged, ranting pasha's daughter whose mission in life is to disturb the peace of all-night coffeehouses; and the younger and even mouthier drunk who sits all day, every day on the stairs of the central train station, who takes such pity on Vasfi one snowy night that she drapes her light green coat over him, not wishing him to die in his sleep. If these characters feel real, it is perhaps because, once upon a time, they were.

Maureen Freely
Bath, England
January 31, 2024

THE PRISONER OF ANKARA

STANDING THERE before the great door, he felt his head begin to spin. But not from joy. For he was drained of all thought and emotion. His mind was blank, his soul numb. An impossible calm had settled over him. How strange it was, to be carried so far on this wave of serenity as to think and feel nothing. To feel as cold as a corpse. Were it not for his heart, he might even have thought himself dead. But his heart was pounding, still very much alive.

For twelve years now, he had been waiting for this moment. Not an hour had passed, not a minute, without his dreaming of it. For twelve long years, he had been waiting for those locked doors to swing open. And each time he had conjured up that moment, he had imagined the joy he'd feel. But now the day had come. One by one the doors had opened. Passing through that last door, he would regain his freedom. No longer a prisoner. A free man once again. Could this be true?

The young gendarme standing guard outside the great door gave him a friendly tap on the shoulder.

"Farewell," he said. "And good luck."

But long after the door had shut behind him, Vasfi was still standing there, in shock. He was no longer in prison! He glanced over at the gendarme, attempting a smile.

The gendarme smiled back. "What are you waiting for, my friend? Time to get going. If I were in your shoes, God forbid, I'd have beat it long ago."

Vasfi reached into his pocket for his cigarettes. He offered one to the gendarme.

"Thanks, brother. But I can't smoke when I'm on duty."

"Take it. You can smoke it later."

"Okay then. How long were you inside, my friend?"

"Twelve years, seven days, and three hours exactly."

The gendarme laughed heartily. Laughed about those last three hours, which may have been the longest and most difficult of Vasfi's entire sentence.

"What's three hours," asked the gendarme, "after twelve whole years?" He spat on the ground and went back to laughing. But how could he be expected to understand—this young fellow who'd seen nothing of life, who had no idea what it meant to be in prison? Vasfi stayed silent. The gendarme kept talking.

"You were inside for a long time, then."

"Yes."

"God grants us patience. Thanks to God's mercy, you have it all behind you now. Once upon a time. Isn't that the way? It's vanished into thin air. Like a fairy tale. Like a dream! And now you're starting life all over. May fortune shine on you, as you set off down the road."

VASFI SHIVERED. Was that what he was, a dead man returned to life? To a new life—though we have only one life to live? His own had been cut in half. But now he would be picking up where he left off. Not to start a new life but, after twelve years of suffering, to continue the old one.

The gendarme waved goodbye, and then Vasfi picked up his bag to head toward the center of this alien city they called Ankara.

Yes, he had lived here for nine years, but with no chance to know the city. He'd spent his first three years in an Istanbul prison. He was moved to Ankara after he was sentenced.

He had no idea what road to take to reach the city center but, held back by a childish fear, he was reluctant to ask for directions. Lest the person he asked might divine, from the first word he uttered, who he was and what he'd just left. How different he felt from everyone else on the street. How could he resemble them in any way? He'd only been outside the prison walls once over the twelve years, and that was when he was taken seriously ill. How does anyone get through a twelve-year sentence? How can a man get through all that without losing his mind? Vasfi had suffered a great deal during his nine years in Ankara. His days here had seemed so much longer. As miserable as he'd been while awaiting trial in Istanbul, and then awaiting each new hearing, he'd held himself together. There'd been his defense to prepare, and after that the appeal. He'd kept himself strong. He'd clung to hope. And his mother, his dear mother—she was still alive then. His brave, kind little mother, who'd never shied away from making the greatest sacrifices for her luckless only son. While she was alive, Vasfi had always felt her standing at his side. Felt the proof of her love, compassionate beyond measure. Even behind that prison's thick walls and unyielding doors, he'd known in his heart that she was there with him, ready to help—spoil him even, as if he were still a child. Every day she'd brought him food she'd cooked herself. Never forgetting his cigarettes. Bringing back, washed and perfectly ironed, the clothes she'd taken away.

After he was sentenced and transferred to Ankara Prison, his mother, not wishing him to feel too alone, had followed him. Before returning home, she'd again given him courage by vowing to do whatever she could to have him moved back to Istanbul.

She'd promised to be back soon, but a few weeks later she'd fallen ill. She'd died in a hospital not long afterward.

When Vasfi was small, his mother liked to tell him that he was destined to become a distinguished doctor. "You'll be the most famous physician this country has ever known. And the most famous professor in a teaching hospital. You'll be the one to look after me when I'm old and weak."

This had been his dear mother's dream for him. A sweet and lovely dream that had not come true on account of one terrible mistake. And he'd been so close. He'd been in medical school with just two years to go when calamity overtook him.

Were it possible to repair the harm he'd caused his mother, he'd have stopped at nothing. He'd have sacrificed anything, just to be at her side when she was dying.

Everything changed after his mother died. He'd never had many visitors. But during the nine years since his mother's death, he'd not had a single one. And how he'd suffered.

On visiting days, everyone else was so cheerful. His fellow prisoners would be busy shaving, combing their hair, sprucing themselves up. While Vasfi just shrank into a corner. For he'd be expecting no one. Every time the guards came in to summon someone, his heart would begin to pound. But all that was in the past now. Those days were over.

Vasfi's gait was slow and troubled. He was free. Those locked doors and impenetrable walls were behind him now. So too were the handcuffs. The gendarmes and the guards. The wardens. The ferocious, carping head guard. All were in the past. As he was leaving, they'd each shaken his hand, offered him advice, encouraging him with a few conciliatory words. Even though these same men had always treated him like their worst enemy, knowing full well that he'd felt the same about them.

Everyone knew that Vasfi was embarking on a new life. The only one who didn't was Vasfi himself. He was still struggling to understand what it meant to not be a prisoner. He wasn't even happy about it. During the nine years he spent despairing inside those luckless walls, he'd thought that only death would free him. It was death he had wished for.

HE WAS walking down straight, bright streets lined by handsome new buildings. On each new street, the same melody poured out through every open window. It was Classical European Music Hour on Ankara Radio. "The head guard must be listening to the same broadcast in his office," Vasfi thought.

His name was Cemal but the other prisoners called him Count. He loved classical European music. It was through him that Vasfi had come to know and love it, too.

He was a middle-aged man. A very cultured one, too, judging by his dignified deportment and way of speaking.

He kept his nails clean, was always freshly shaven. Even in the blue-gray uniforms they made the prisoners wear, he looked elegant and well-dressed. To look at him, no one would know he'd murdered a four-year-old girl for no apparent reason. Possibly just for the thrill of the kill. He was still awaiting his sentence. "He'll probably hang," Vasfi thought. "But I've served my sentence," he said out loud. "I'm free. I'm no longer in prison."

True enough. He was no longer in prison. But his thoughts kept returning to it. Impossible to put those twelve wretched years behind him.

The names and faces of his friends inside had changed all the time. But whatever they looked like, whatever their names, they had been his equals.

They'd all belonged to the same world . . . and Vasfi had grown accustomed to them.

"I'm a murderer, too . . ." This thought sent a shiver through him. As if to jar him awake. "I'm a murderer, too."

In prison, in the company of so many other murderers, his own crime had not seemed unusually frightening. But now, in this world to which he had just returned, to look at the people around him and think of himself as a murderer was a torment he could barely endure.

Seeing a wide avenue ahead, he thought, "First things first. Let's find a hotel." One of his fellow inmates, Veznedar Nazmi Bey, had lived in Ankara for a long time. He'd given Vasfi the address of a small hotel near Anafartalar Avenue. Vasfi conjured up his face. A fat, short, red-cheeked accountant, inside for embezzlement. Always ready to tell his story.

"He'll be with Big Şefkati, now," Vasfi thought. "And Muslihittin Hodja, and Artin the Artist." His own place in that circle left empty. They were probably sad and on edge tonight, these friends who, for an hour now, had ceased to be his fellow inmates.

It was like that every time someone was released. In the days leading up to it, the mood in the cells would lighten. And when there was only one day left, there was joy. All the inmates would be cheered by the thought of their friend's imminent release. It felt almost like a festival. And when the day arrived, they'd walk the lucky man to the door, showering him with blessings, wishing him peace and the best of luck. And then, as he walked on, they'd call after him: "May God protect you from further misfortune!"

But as soon as their friend had left and all the doors closed again, their faces would fall. They'd do their best to laugh and joke, but it was an act. They'd each be counting the years, months, and hours still to be served.

On nights like this, they'd hide behind their pride, each thinking himself alone in the world. Each thinking how empty the dormitories and corridors.

Vasfi was only too familiar with this sad ritual. How many times had he accompanied a fellow prisoner to that last door, wishing him all the best, but once the man had been set free and that same door had closed, cruelly preventing his own release, he'd sink into despondency. So yes, the friends he'd left behind were sad tonight.

They'd probably lost their courage. Vasfi felt his heart wrenching. It was almost as if he felt guilty about leaving his friends behind.

Every evening at five o'clock, Veznedar Nazmi would brew up a coffee. Sometimes he would share it with his inmates. Tonight they'd be gathering as they always did, and they'd be talking about Vasfi. And trying to look cheerful, of course. This would be easier for Nazmi than it would for the others. He had only six months left. Muslihittin Hodja still had seven years to serve. As for Artin—the poor man was sixty years old. He wouldn't be getting out until he was eighty. He'd sacrificed his freedom for the woman he called his Lovely. Remembering that now, Vasfi couldn't help but smile. He knew her from Artin's paintings, and from the photograph that Artin carried with him and was always showing people. He'd sketch her likeness on bits of paper, and on canvas if he could find it, and on the walls and the doors—whatever surface he could find. His beloved was not at all lovely. But Artin had worshipped her, and in a mad and savage burst of jealousy he had killed her.

NOW VASFI was at a crossroads. He stopped to look around him. "Soon these people will be returning to their homes," he thought, "where others will be waiting for them. They know where they're going." That was why they were in such a hurry. Vasfi had nowhere to go, and no one waiting for him. All he had in this alien city where he knew not a soul was the piece of paper in his hand, with the address of a hotel.

Through mournful eyes he watched the crowds around him. "Shall I ever grow accustomed to living among these people?" he asked himself.

He kept walking, until he could walk no more. That hotel where he'd be spending his first night of freedom—he needed to find it at once. "Or shall I go straight to the station?" he wondered. "Would it be better to just jump on a train and head back to Istanbul?" He dismissed the idea at once. "It makes no sense to leave for Istanbul before I've had a chance to see this city that's been my home for nine years now, without my having seen any part of it. And it's not as if I have anyone waiting for me in Istanbul."

Suddenly he realized why he felt so low on the day of his long-waited release.

He needed to find his way to the hotel. Looking around him, he caught sight of a young woman at a bus stop, and his heart lifted as his cheeks began to burn.

"She looks so much like Zeynep!" he thought. She was tall and slim, black-eyed and olive-skinned.

THEY PUT him into a room with four beds. The porter went over to the window and opened it.

"The two beds on the left are taken," he said. "You can take either of the ones on the right."

"I'd like the bed by the window."

"Certainly."

The porter was a short man whose pointed nose called to mind a fox. On his way out, he stopped by the door.

"You don't look like you're from around here."

"No, I'm not from Ankara."

"Ankara's a beautiful city."

"Yes, it is."

"Is this your first time here?"

Vasfi paused for a moment, uncertain what to say. "Yes," he finally replied.

"There's a licensed restaurant just across the street. They have good wines, and the food's not bad either."

"Thank you."

"Across the street there's a bigger, cleaner restaurant. But they don't serve alcohol. If you're feeling tired and want to stay in, I can fetch you a sandwich from the cafeteria on the corner."

"Thank you. But I'll be heading out in a moment. I'd like to see a bit of the city."

"As you wish."

After the man left the room, Vasfi felt as relieved as if he'd just been delivered from a terrible toothache. The noise of the city had tired him out, as had walking all that distance, in shoes. His feet were throbbing. He sat down on his bed, pushing his bag underneath it. There he sat for a long time, his mind blank, and his heart hollow.

This was a prison habit: to sit very still and wait for nothing in particular. Numb to the passing hours . . .

By the time he came back to himself, night had fallen. He must, he thought with alarm, have been sitting there for two hours.

"I have nothing left in common with normal people," he thought. But he had to make an effort. "No matter, I'll find a way to adjust. Learn to live like a free man again."

But somewhere deep inside him, another Vasfi was shaking his head: "No, no . . . what's done is done—you're never going back to the Vasfi you once were."

With effort he stood up, to shuffle as far as the sink. Looking into the mirror hanging above it, he saw a pale and weary man with a creased forehead.

"I look like a corpse just risen from the grave," he thought. "Am I doomed to carry my prison years with me, wherever I go? Will I never go back to being the man I was?"

It was very late by the time Vasfi reached the coffeehouse. He found himself a place in the corner. He felt so tired by the time he'd finished his tea that he had no choice but to lean on the table and take his heavy, throbbing head in his hands.

He wasn't asleep. He could still hear people coming and going, and someone snoring at the next table. He'd had plenty to drink but almost nothing to eat. Stroking his forehead, he thought, "Maybe I could doze off, too." He closed his eyes. "I can't sleep, can't think. No release for me, ever!"

He made an effort to conjure up an image of Zeynep. Dear Zeynep. Oh, how he'd loved her. No one could match her. It was a struggle to bring her back into his mind, but at last he succeeded. And then there she was, sitting right across from him—tall, slender, and irresistible. Such joy in those eyes. They could drive a man mad.

Vasfi kept his eyes closed, fearing that if he opened them, he might lose her. She was sitting on a swing, young and agile, swaying back and forth, first slowly, but gradually gaining speed. Up and down she went, faster and faster. Changing before his eyes with each descent. Until suddenly, in the place of the old Zeynep, a new Zeynep took her place. This new Zeynep was vulgar and fat. She was flashing her golden teeth and grinning at him hatefully. What a terrible sight. Vasfi wanted to open his eyes, bring this nightmare to an end. But he couldn't. He was asleep, he knew he was asleep. Knew he was dreaming. But he couldn't move his arms. His every limb so heavy and broken. He sank back into his nightmare, moaning.

Life was against him. The old Zeynep was gone, never to return.

"What's wrong? Can I help you?"

He felt a hand on his shoulder, and when he turned to look at it, he saw it belonged to a woman. His eyes moved to her wrist and her shoulder, traveling upward until at last he saw her face. He recognized her at once. The dark woman from the next table. She was wearing an old green wool jacket. Her eyes were green, too. Even in this half-light, they were as bright as spring. She had a lovely voice, this woman. "All women's voices must be this beautiful," he told himself.

So where was he now, this man he once was?

The man he was now could hardly remember him. All he could hold in his mind was a vague sketch.

He had no idea how to get the two Vasfis to connect. No way to understand what had driven him to madness. When he thought about the man he'd once been, he felt neither hatred nor resentment, sympathy nor compassion.

While at the same time he wanted to believe he was still the same man. He needed to believe this, absolutely. Without that belief, he'd never overcome his grief. Or at least, if he was to live at all, he needed to believe that his feelings for Zeynep remained constant. This was more than just necessary; it was crucial. "If I sacrificed my life, I sacrificed it for Zeynep." That's what the old Vasfi had said, and what a consolation it would be, could be, if the new Vasfi could say the same.

But though the new Vasfi could still utter these words, they lacked their old fire and conviction. For the old Vasfi, nothing had been good enough for Zeynep. He'd always wanted the best and most beautiful he could find for her ... And now, just as then, he needed to believe that the sacrifices he'd made for Zeynep were justified. His memories of her were sacrosanct. Without them, his life would have no meaning. He would lose the courage to live.

He had sacrificed everything for Zeynep: his life, his youth, his most beautiful years. He'd loved her madly. Worshipped her. He was trying to convince himself that he still loved her with his old intensity. But Zeynep was no more than a faint dream for him now. A dream that bore only a vague resemblance to the old one. He tried to conjure her up again—her flashing teeth and her intoxicating smile. The gorgeous laugh still ringing in his ears. That slender waist, those long, smooth legs, those black eyes so alive with promise, as bright as stars on a summer night.

But no matter how hard he tried, the details eluded him. The colors faded.

He was back in his room now. The door flew open. Vasfi looked up to see a stout man come inside.

"Hello!" the man said.

"Hello!"

"Sorry. I'd have knocked if I'd known you were here."

"Please. There was no need."

The man took off his hat, threw it onto his bed, and sat down beside it. "You've just arrived, I take it."

"Yes. I just got here."

"I stepped out three hours ago exactly, and you'd not yet arrived."

"Yes, that's true."

"Did you just come in from Istanbul?"

"No."

"But you're clearly from Istanbul. I could see that right away."

"Yes, I'm from Istanbul, and I intend to return."

"How could anyone from a city as beautiful as Istanbul ever live in any other? You must have tried everything in your power to stay there."

To fend off any more questions, Vasfi went over to the sink to wash his hands. But his roommate carried on talking.

"So you really are from Istanbul, and what a beautiful city it is, too. I know it well, I've been there a few times. I stayed in a lovely hotel in Sirkeci, most times . . ."

"This man is never going to shut up," Vasfi thought.

The man continued talking. "I had some good times there. So much to see! And the women—they're pretty nice, too . . ." Turning to Vasfi with a silly smile, he said. "Aren't they just?

"You're right. They are. Are you from Ankara?"

"No, but I spend half the year here. I have a wife in Keskin. And a mill."

After drying his hands, Vasfi picked up his hat.

"Are you going out?" asked the man.

"Yes."

"Where are you headed—Çiftlik or Bomonti? Those are the only two places where you can eat well in Ankara."

Vasfi gave no answer.

"I'd recommend Çiftlik. It's not close by, but if you hop into a taxi you'll be there in no time."

"Is that so?"

"I was thinking of going there myself tonight, actually. They have pretty good singers. And the girls—each one more beautiful than the last, thank God. Of course, that'll mean nothing to you. You're used to the beauties of Istanbul. But you should still go to Çiftlik. You won't regret it."

"Maybe I'll try it out," said Vasfi with a smile. But he knew he'd never go to such a place, he had no taste for those places and no patience for their high prices. With no friends or relatives to depend on, he was going to have to live on the money in his pocket until he found work. He turned to the man, who was still had the same smile plastered on his face.

"Goodbye for now."

"Goodbye."

He left the room, closing the door softly behind him.

HE LINGERED for a time on the sidewalk, to get his bearings. It wasn't too late yet. Night had not yet fallen. He thought about what he'd been doing this time yesterday. He'd been about to share his last meal with his friends in misfortune. Muslihittin Hodja would be out in the courtyard with his brazier, cooking pilaf for supper. No one could stop him cooking his rice, not even the prison authorities. He was a hodja, after all. The guards pretended not to notice this little whim of his.

Muslihittin Hodja took great stock in this dispensation, and he cooked his evening pilaf with loving care. He consumed it with gusto, smacking his lips as he ate. When Vasfi could bear the noise no longer, he'd say, "If you keep on smacking your lips like that, I'm going to smack your face." The hodja never took offense at these words. "You're right, my son," he'd say. "What can I do? I got this bad habit during the year I spent in solitary. I came to enjoy hearing what I ate. It made me feel like I wasn't alone in that cell."

The hodja had a thin face and a short beard. There was a red mark on his left cheek. When he spoke you could see all his teeth, which had a green tint to them, plus his gums, which were white. He had a modest manner and never picked fights. He was humble. But despite all this, Muslihittin Hodja was a murderer. He was serving twenty years for poisoning his wife. The hodja refused all responsibility. He would seize every opportunity to say so. "I didn't kill my wife," he would say. "She died by drinking poison." He could not have believed his own words. Muslihittin Hodja was an original. He never stayed in the same prison for long. Whenever he grew tired of where he was, he'd begin making inquiries. Somehow or other, he'd get himself transferred to another prison.

He also had plans for the future. When he was in the right mood, he'd share them: "The first thing I'll do when I get out of here? Find myself a young wife. An innocent, purehearted little girl . . ."

Yes, Muslihittin Hodja could talk about his plans. He already knew what he'd be doing once he was released. Whereas there hadn't been a day inside when Vasfi had managed to convince himself that one day he'd be free.

No doubt this explained why he was so troubled and confused now that he had put prison behind him.

With hesitant steps he entered the little restaurant on the corner. Its tablecloths did not look so very clean. But still they looked good to Vasfi: For the first time in twelve years, he was going to eat at a table with a tablecloth. He headed over to an empty table. It was quite crowded in the restaurant. The waiter didn't see him right away. But Vasfi was happy to wait.

With the patience he'd acquired in prison, he looked around him. Almost none of the customers were women. Almost all were men. The owner, a fat man, was seated behind the cash register. There was a melancholy old song on the radio. Vasfi knew this plaintive folk song very well. Mahmut the Musician would sing it so often that Şefkati, losing patience, would cry out, "Why do you always have to pour all this pain on us. You're destroying us, man! This is not the Akıntı Burnu Meyhane. You're in a prison. Shut up now. We're sick to death of that song."

Everyone would laugh, while Mahmut, pretending to have heard nothing, would carry on singing. A strange man, this Mahmut. He didn't mind insults. He didn't even mind curses. Nothing bothered him. He had neither self-respect nor dignity, and no fight in him. Never did he talk back. One thing is sure, thought Vasfi, Mahmut will be singing that song tonight, and Şefkati will again be railing against him: "The doors of the Akıntı Burnu Meyhane will never open again for you or for me . . . and do you know why? We're both notorious!"

Poor Şefkati, always losing his temper. His nerves were shot. He'll argue with the guards about the lights tonight . . . Like every night.

It made Vasfi wonder. Only the first years of prison had been hard to bear. That must be it. But slowly he'd found some peace. Sometimes he'd object to something, but before long he'd have handed himself back to God's will. When you handed yourself over to God, though, didn't that mean surrendering all the feelings that made you human? That must be it. Slowly but surely, a prisoner surrendered all his feelings. Sank into lethargy and slumber. In the end, a prisoner became a shadow of his former self. Prisoners were people without souls. This was worse than being dead.

Time now to wake himself up. Go in search of what he had once thought of as his soul and rouse it. No, this couldn't happen fast. No one could stop feeling dead in an instant. It was going to be a hard slog, this he knew.

Suddenly he blanched.

The radio was playing an old folk song called "My Zeynep": "*My Zeynep, the talk of three villages.*" She might have been beautiful, this girl, but his own Zeynep was more beautiful still.

The waiter had yet to take his order. So he stood up and raced to the door. He wanted to leave that folk song behind. But it followed him out into the street. The radio in the coffeehouse across the street was playing the same song.

He walked down a few streets, stopping finally in front of a small meyhane. Walking inside, he went over to the bar and ordered a rakı. It was very dark inside this place. The manager stared at him with his one good eye. With his dirty hands he served him a glass of rakı and a few simple mezes.

This being his first drink in years, Vasfi felt his head spinning from the first sip.

There was no radio here. There were two workmen laughing and joking at one end of the bar. At the other there were three students having an argument. Between him and them, there was a disheveled, red-eyed man holding his glass to his lips.

After his first glass, Vasfi felt calmer. He ordered a second glass and smoked a cigarette. Then he made his slow way back to the hotel and went straight to bed.

His roommates were still out. Vasfi had the room to himself. He couldn't get to sleep. He repeated the same sentence to himself, over and over: "Tomorrow I shall return to Istanbul." But then other thoughts intruded. "Will I find the courage to go in search of Zeynep?" He was certain he never would. "I wonder how much she's changed? Is my great-uncle still alive?" Twelve years ago, the great-uncle in question was already very old.

It did not matter to him if Zeynep had changed or not. Today, like every other day, he could not remember how she looked. It was as if her face had been erased from his mind. What sort of woman had she been? All he could remember of that tall, slender, black-eyed woman was the childish way she threw her head back when she laughed. And the laugh itself—so full of joy at times, and so teasing and provocative at others. On the day he'd first heard it, he'd been lying in bed. A summer day. The window that looked onto the small garden was open. He'd been unable to sleep. But the heat had worn him out. The afternoon heat bore down on him. He was lying in bed with his eyes closed. Then suddenly he'd heard that extraordinary laugh. So wild and so joyous. At once his eyes had opened. It was a woman's laugh. But it had the purity and joy of a child's. Who was this woman who still knew how to laugh from the heart?

Vasfi knew everyone in this small neighborhood. The gardens on the block on which he lived were separated from each other by wooden fences. He stood up and went to the window to take a look at this woman who could laugh so beautifully, but he couldn't see her.

In one of the little gardens, four children were playing tag. In another, an old woman was feeding her cat. In the garden across the way, Nuriye Hanım was washing clothes. The laughter continued. It was, he decided, coming from the house just opposite his own. From Nuriye Hanım's three-story house. Nuriye Hanım lived on the ground floor. The other two she rented out.

On the first floor was a retired clerk named Faruk Bey and his wife. A gloomy couple, weighed down by their ailments. No one in the neighborhood had ever seen them so much as smile. A mother and daughter lived on the second floor. They both worked in the same tire factory. Both were on the night shift. They'd leave the house at eight in the evening and return the next morning at seven. A nervous, sullen pair. They'd go straight to bed when they got home and sleep all day. Their curtains were always closed. A woman had lived alone on the third floor, but she'd died, and her windows had been closed ever since.

But today, he now noticed, that one of those windows was open again. And through that window he could hear a very familiar creaking. Someone inside was scrubbing the floorboards. With water and soap, just like his mother did. It struck him as strange, how someone could be laughing while undertaking such a taxing and tiring task. This was, after all, a neighborhood where joy was in short supply.

FROM THAT day on, Vasfi could not get that laugh out of his mind. He heard it at all hours. Each and every time it burned its way through his heart. This laugh that carried inside it the warmth of a flickering flame.

Vasfi was still a young man then. Innocent and inexperienced, and like all those his age, easily stirred up.

Vasfi had never known a father's firm hand. His mother, who adored her son, had never treated him harshly. Vasfi had spent seven years at his first school, instead of the usual five. His favorite pastime, when he wasn't playing ball with friends, was to go into the fields and set lime traps for birds. At fourteen he'd thought himself a grown-up. He'd already started smoking. By seventeen he was drinking with his friends at the local meyhanes. Even so, that laughter cast a spell on him.

He was still a lycée student when he had his first romantic adventure. The girl was a lycée student like him, so it went no further than an exchange of letters. Fine words written by children.

Not long afterward, the beautiful wife of the neighborhood butcher had invited Vasfi to visit when her husband was away. A tiny, pink-skinned blond woman. The liaison continued for several months. Then the butcher expanded his business, moving his operations to the Spice Bazaar and his wife to a house in another part of the city. Thereafter it became very difficult for Vasfi to see her. With that, he decided to give her up. By now he considered himself a man of the world, who knew life for what it was and had tired of it.

Around this time, he considered dropping out of school to take up work in a small business. His mother did everything in her power to stop him. Since being widowed she'd been cleaning rich people's houses, so that her son could continue his education.

"No my child," she'd say. "You'll continue with your education. This is what I want for you. You don't have to work until you've earned your degree. I'm only working because your father's pension doesn't cover our expenses. And because I want you to finish your education, like your father and your grandfather before you."

Whereupon Vasfi would embrace his mother. And tease her. "So tell me, darling Mother, what sort of education did my grandfather have?"

"You're right, he never studied at a university. He was just an artisan. But so very talented! He could be counted as an artist—"

"Mother dear, my grandfather was a carpenter, no more than that. Just like my great-uncle."

"Don't say that, my son, you've seen what your grandfather made. How can you talk about your uncle in the same breath? He has none of your grandfather's skill or mastery."

"Never mind, little Mother. Even if my uncle did have Grandfather's mastery, what difference would it make? Look at my father's uncle—he didn't get an education, nor did he have his brother's skills, but that didn't stop him from becoming the richest person in our family."

"Just forget about your great-uncle, my child. He's in business. He's had that shop in the central market for a very long time. Of course he'll have lots of money."

"Inevitably. As we all know."

"I want you to be something better than a rich businessman. I want you to use your brain. My father was a humble teacher—and a gentleman, to be sure. Very intelligent, and well read, too. Your father, too. He was just a modest civil servant. And he saw a great future for you. 'I don't want my son to follow in my footsteps,' he'd say. 'He has it in him to be a scholar, or even a distinguished doctor.'"

She would smile whenever she spoke like this, her face flushing with pleasure.

"Yes, my son," she'd say, "I want you to become a doctor. A great doctor. I know how brilliant you are. So who knows, you could even become a famous doctor. That's what you could become, if you put your mind to it. When I'm a tired old woman, you'll be the one to look after me. You'll take care of me. I'm still young now, I still have the strength to work. So I shall work and you shall study, and I shall take on the hardest tasks gladly. After that, you will support us both. It will be your turn to work."

She made such an effort that in the end he agreed to continue his studies. Having decided to become a doctor, as his mother wished, he began to study in earnest.

AT THE time he fell under the spell of the invisible woman with the joyously childish laugh, he was a medical student. He was twenty years old, and he couldn't get that laugh out of his mind. He kept a watch on that third-floor window in the house just opposite, but he never managed to see the woman whose laugh so entranced him.

Until one day, when he heard her laughing in the little garden of the house opposite their own. He also heard the squeaking of a swing. He rushed to the window to see two young girls in the garden. One was on the swing and the other was standing in the doorway.

They were chattering away and laughing. The girl in the doorway was tiny and blond; the one on the swing was slim, long-legged, and dark-skinned. Her mass of curly hair was as black as night. With every downward swing, it all flew up into the air. When her skirt did the same, he could see her beautiful bronze legs. Up and down she went, higher and higher, to vanish behind the leaves of the tree. How happy these girls were. Until the blond girl caught sight of Vasfi and whispered something to her friend. Whereupon the dark girl cast a sarcastic glance in Vasfi's direction, before turning to her friend to laugh. Vasfi recognized it at once—that bold, enchanting, provocative laugh that had robbed him of so many nights of sleep. The girl kept swinging, turning now and again to look at Vasfi. Then she jumped off her swing to take her friend by the hand. As they walked through the door, she turned around to smile at him—fearlessly, flirtatiously, but sweetly, too.

VASFI WAS stunned but also elated to see she was as he'd imagined her. He'd not thought she'd be so tall. He'd always known she'd be dark and attractive, but he'd never imagined she'd be as beautiful as this.

On the day he first saw her, he did not stay long in his mother's room. He returned to his own, and before he'd turned on his lamp or even lit a cigarette, he ran to the window to watch the house opposite. Only the first-floor lights were on. All the upper windows were dark.

For an hour, he just stood there, his eyes glued to the windows across the way.

After an hour his patience was rewarded. One of the windows in the house opposite lit up, and he could see a woman in shadow. It was her. She'd tied up her bountiful hair in a bun. She was wandering around the room.

When she drew close to the window, he could see her from the shoulders up. When she drew away, she disappeared altogether. All Vasfi could see was the huge ghostly shadow she cast on the back wall. From her gestures, he could tell she was undressing.

She had no idea she was being watched by her curious neighbor. She returned to the window to linger for a moment or two, and then she walked away to turn off the lamp. "Now she's in her bed," he thought. "Who can say how lovely that dark body must look against those white sheets." His own body warmed at the thought. "How hot it is tonight," he thought, as he left the window.

The heat was truly overwhelming. Vasfi's heart was pounding. He was bathed in sweat.

"A person could drown in this house," he murmured. The same could be said of every house in this neighborhood. They sat in the sun all day long, these wooden houses. And then, at night, that hellish heat kept pressing in. The sea was close by, but it offered them no solace. Its sweet breezes never found their way through the narrow streets of this poor neighborhood.

Vasfi turned on his lamp. He wanted to read. But he was unable to concentrate.

He was thirsty, so he went downstairs for a glass of water. These houses had their kitchens on the ground floor, all leading into small halls. In addition to the front door, there was a door leading out into the garden.

Vasfi found his mother and two neighbors sitting at the round table. They'd left both doors open, to let in some air.

His mother's guests—Nuriye Hanım and Esma Hanım—greeted Vasfi.

"Can I get you anything, my son?"

"I'm thirsty, Mother."

"I hung a basket in the cistern. There's a bottle of water in there, it should be cold. Take it from there."

"Thanks, Mother."

Entering the kitchen, he walked straight over to the garden door and, placing his arms on either side of it, looked out at the houses across the way. It was cooler down here than in his room. While he stood there, he listened to what Nuriye Hanım was saying to his mother.

"Şükran Hanım, you are a very lucky woman to have such a child. Thanks be to God!"

"I do always thank God, my dear Nuriye Hanım, and I truly am a lucky woman."

"When you get to my age, you won't have to struggle, you'll have your son to look after you."

"If God wills it, sister."

"If God wills it," echoed Esma.

"It's hard to live alone with no hand to help you. Only those who have done so can understand."

Nuriye Hanım fell silent for a time. With a sigh, she began to speak again: "A hand is always a hand. However much good you do, you still have your own hand to help you. People are ungrateful. Look at the gentleman and his good wife. Mahmure Hanım could have shown a bit more gratitude."

"Yes, yes," said Vasfi's mother. "We all know how well you looked after her when she was ill. You couldn't have done more if she'd been your own sister."

"And did she ever improve? She's still poorly. I still do her house day in, day out."

"Nuriye Hanım has a heart of gold," Esma Hanım said as she sighed. "I'd never make such sacrifices for a stranger."

Again Nuriye Hanım sighed. "As you know, I'm an odd one, I live alone. I've known Mahmure Hanım for forty years. We want to reach out to such people, to love them. I loved her like a sister, I did everything I could for her. But she did everything in her power to poison my life."

"Tell me again what she did?" Esma said.

"As I said already: She's ungrateful. And now she's upset by these arguments between Besime and her mother. God knows how it's upset me."

"Dear oh dear," said Şükran Hanım, his mother.

In a tearful voice, Nuriye continued: "It was because they were arguing so much that she said I had to evict them. Mahmure Hanım wants this from me. What's it to me if they argue? They're not arguing with me! If they're tearing each other's hair out in their own room, it's no concern of mine. They're my best tenants. They've never once been late with the rent. On the first of the month, bam, there it is."

"You're right, my dear neighbor," Esma agreed.

"If someone is inconvenienced by noise in a humble boardinghouse like mine, they should consider moving to their own apartment, or a private house, or a mansion!"

"You're so right, dear neighbor," Esma agreed.

"She's been giving me the silent treatment ever since I told her that I wasn't going to ask Mahmure Hanım to leave. She won't even wish me good day."

"It's shocking," said Esma. "Truly it is. You have your own bills to pay, it's not as if you own the whole world."

"Bless you, Esma Hanım. I like Besime and her mother. They're very fine women. They were both out of work all last winter, but they never fell behind with the rent. No mattresses to lie on, no clothes in their closets. But they're in debt to no one. Besime even sold that beautiful wool coat of hers for a song. I felt so bad that I told them they could wait on paying the rent until they had work again. But they refused. By God, I haven't a harsh word to say about them. And neither can I do them any harm."

"You're an angel, Nuriye Hanım," said Esma.

"This isn't about being good. It's about being humane. I try to be humane with everyone. If I am then met with ingratitude, I can help feeling angry. I find ingratitude intolerable. But you know what's really getting to me? After all I've done for Besime and her mother, they've begun grumbling too. They have no idea that others have been complaining about them, but now they're complaining about the new tenants."

Vasfi had only been half listening up to this point, but now he pricked up his ears.

"Who are these new tenants of yours?" Esma asked. "No one in the neighborhood knows them, they must be new to these parts."

"Yes, they moved here from Edirnekapı or thereabouts. The man is a cook, he works at a kebab shop somewhere near Fındıklı. A little shed of a place. His wife goes there with him, to help out. They leave every morning at dawn and come back very late."

"Then what are Besime and her mother complaining about seeing as they themselves work nights?"

"It's not the parents that are making the noise. It's their daughter."

"Is she very young, this daughter?"

"Not young at all! She's fully grown, this girl, and a real beauty, but she doesn't know how to behave. She's a wild thing. Raucous. Won't listen to anyone. Always blowing off steam."

"Doesn't she work?"

Nuriye Hanım pursed her lips at Esma's question.

"Oh, children today, do they ever spare a thought for their elders? Her parents wear themselves out working, while she sits at home pleasing herself. Putting her feet up, as they say. That's what young people are like these days. Inviting their friends over, listening to the gramophone, singing, making a ruckus. She's a giddy gadabout of a thing, I mean to say. Like so many young people today, she can't even see the floor beneath her feet. And she has the loudest laugh."

When he heard the word "laugh," Vasfi felt a warm current passing through him.

"You're right, Nuriye Hanım," said his mother. "From the ground to the sky, you are right. Young people have the right to laugh. Didn't we all laugh a little, and get up to a bit of mischief, and make noise when we were their age?"

Vasfi was shocked to hear his mother say this. It had never occurred to him that once upon a time she might have been as joyful as this new neighbor, or that she could have laughed like her. It seemed impossible. He could not recall her ever having laughed at all. Her face exuded a lovely innocence, but her usual expression was mournful and downcast.

Passing through the hall on his way up to his room, he wrapped his arms around her narrow shoulders and said, "God bless you, dear Mother."

"And you, my child."

As he went upstairs to his room, he heard Nuriye Hanım say, "May God protect your son, and may He give all mothers sons as devoted as yours. Şükran Hanım, you must be the happiest woman in the world."

"Yes," said his mother sweetly. "I truly am."

Vasfi went into his room and closed his door behind him.

FOR THREE long weeks, Vasfi thought about the neighbor girl day and night. He longed to see her, meet her, talk with her. From time to time, he caught sight of her in the window, trying to guess her habits, and her comings and goings, so that he might contrive a meeting.

The girl saw him watching her, and this pleased her. She seemed to come up to the window just so that he could see her. If their eyes met, she would smile.

One day he found the courage to admit to himself that he liked the girl a great deal. A few days later, he was admitting to himself that he'd never liked any girl quite as much.

He couldn't sleep. His exams were approaching but Vasfi didn't care. Just one thought was running through his head: "I have to meet her, I have to meet her, until I meet her, I shall know no peace."

Finally he decided that the next time he saw her leave the house, he would follow after her, catch up with her, and speak to her.

One day she came to the window, smiled at him, and shut the window. From this Vasfi understood that she was leaving the house, so he rushed out too, turned the corner into her street, and there she was. Rapidly he

34

approached her. She was wearing a red dress. Vulgar though it was, it only served to accentuate her beauty.

Her mass of shiny black curls fell to her shoulders. She was wearing a thick metal bracelet that had been spray-painted gold, and a turquoise ring in a fussy setting. Even so, Vasfi found her enchanting. And so beautiful as to make his heart race. She'd cast such a spell over him that he'd lost the courage to speak. The young girl carried on walking, turning around from time to time to look at Vasfi. In this way they left their narrow street to come out onto a wide avenue. Vasfi was still following her, but not daring to address her.

"I have to say something, or I'll look like a fool," he told himself. But he couldn't think what to say. "Where to begin? What's the right thing to say first? She's no different from the other neighborhood girls!" Even though she was. As Vasfi was soon to find out.

They'd gone a long way down the avenue by now. Vasfi still tongue-tied and ashamed. Finally he increased his pace, determined to speak to her, but once he found himself at her side, he again lost his courage and walked past her instead. He was two or three steps ahead when he heard her call out in a joyous, mocking voice, "Hey, neighbor! Where are you going in such a hurry?"

Shocked, Vasfi looked back at her. The avenue was quite empty. There was no one around them. In a trembling voice, he asked, "Are you talking to me?"

The young girl let out a peal of laughter. "I'm certainly not talking to myself!"

And Vasfi laughed with her. "I am very happy for you to talk to me."

"If it were left to you, you'd never have found the courage."

"Even though . . ." He could say no more.

"Even though you followed me here so you could speak to me."

"Yes, you've made a good guess."

"I didn't guess it. I saw it with my own eyes." She fell silent for a moment, and then she added, "I've been seeing it with my own eyes for three weeks now, in fact. You've been watching me at my window the way a cat looks at a lung in the butcher's shop. Which would be fine if it was just me, but the whole neighborhood has noticed. They've even started gossiping about us."

"Why? What did I do to deserve that?"

"What more could you do? If it keeps on going like this, you might even guess my name." She frowned, casting him a wrathful look. "Look at me now. Even a wolf doesn't eat his neighbor, as they say."

"I'm not a wolf, and—"

"And you don't eat people, is that what you were going to say? Maybe not, but—"

"All I've done is look at you, what's wrong with that? If I can't take my eyes off your window, it's because you're so beautiful. So very beautiful . . ."

"You do more than just stare at my window. Today you followed me. Who can know what you'll do tomorrow. But know this. Not every bird is for eating."

"You're welcome."

"Shut your mouth. Don't tell me fairy tales. I know what you're after, and that's why I've decided to speak to you. I'm afraid of gossip, do you hear?"

"Am I guilty of a crime? What have I done for you to scold me so?"

"You are indeed guilty of a crime. So pardon me if I don't thank you!"

"Please forgive me . . . I never imagined—"

"Never imagined that I didn't want to become the talk of the neighborhood?"

"No, that's not what I meant to say."

"In that case, why don't you tell me what you did mean to say."

"I never imagined that anyone could see me while I was admiring you at the window. Because I was standing away from the window so that no one else could see me."

"I'm going to speak openly with you now. I don't want you watching me from your window. I don't want people talking! I don't want the neighborhood witches uttering my name!"

"I shouldn't watch you from my window anymore— is that what you're saying?"

"That would be better for both of us. If nothing else, you could start studying for your exams."

"You're talking like we're enemies—"

"Why enemies?"

"If I can't see you, I can't go on living."

"Oh come now. What were you doing before now? We're new to the neighborhood."

"I didn't know you then."

"And now we're friends? You still don't know me."

"No, I don't know you. But I want to know you."

"Window to window. You've been ogling me. And where does that leave me? Is that any way to get to know someone?"

"Of course not. And now that you've told me you have no interest in knowing me, it's out of the question. But please, if nothing else, give me permission to watch you from my window just once in a while. If I can't see you—believe me, I'll fall apart. I'll be so miserable!"

"Then try to find another way to see me."

"Another way?"

"How old are you, little lamb?"

"Twenty-two."

"Tell me another one. You act like a foolish eight-year-old boy."

"Foolish?"

"That's what I said. Any other twenty-two-year-old would find a way to talk to a girl he fancied without alerting the whole neighborhood." She winked, and then smiled. "I know what I would do, if I were you."

"Then tell me."

The young girl put her small hand on Vasfi's shoulder, and in a jubilant voice, she said, "Come on now, you idiot. What's keeping you from asking me out to the movies?"

TOGETHER THEY walked into the cinema. For Vasfi this was unexpected bliss. When the theater went dark, he tried to hold the girl's hand, but she pulled it away.

"Listen, neighbor boy," she hissed into his ear. "Keep your hands to yourself. I don't like that kind of thing. If you try that again, our first trip to the movies will be our last."

He didn't try again. He didn't dare.

As they left the cinema, Vasfi said, "I still don't know your name. May I ask what it is?"

"My name is Zeynep. Do you like it?"

"I like it very much."

SO THAT'S how the story started—in the simple, vulgar way so common among young people in the city's poorer neighborhoods. From that day on, they went out together many times—sometimes to films, sometimes to pudding shops and pastry shops. Oftentimes they took strolls in a park. From time to time, Vasfi found enough courage to take hold of the girl's hand and stroke it. But every time he did, she pulled roughly away.

"Now listen, neighbor boy," she'd say. "You will stop this nonsense or else. If you don't, you'll never see me again."

Sometimes, if they were on an empty street, Vasfi would try to stroke her hair or put his arm around her waist, and she'd turn harsh.

"I'm a serious girl," she'd say. "I demand respect."

And then would come the threat: "If you keep it up, you'll never see me again. Not even the tips of my fingernails."

And Vasfi would apologize. Fearing he might never see her again, he would promise not to touch her. But afterward, when he was alone again, he would go into a quiet rage. "She's mocking me," he'd think. "Making a fool of me, treating me like a child. Laughing in my face." Why did he love this girl so much anyway? She wasn't overly intelligent. She had a coarse way of talking and a vulgar, simpleminded way of thinking. She dressed badly, and she didn't seem to know how brush her hair. But in spite of all this, he thought her more beautiful than any other.

Vasfi thought little of Zeynep's moral values. He looked down on her, thought himself superior. One moment they'd be laughing and joking, and the next moment, he'd lose his temper and start ranting. Raging. Vasfi would later regret his words. He was losing his self-respect. But whenever she had upset him the most, Zeynep would finish the day by suddenly becoming all sweetness and light. She would clear the air with a cheerful word, a little joke. Do whatever she could to part on good terms. And Vasfi would relent. There were times, though, when he was already too angry to stop shouting. Zeynep never took his rages too seriously. She'd just laugh and change the subject.

It was always when he felt happiest to have Zeynep at his side that she'd say something to break his heart and plunge him into despair.

While Zeynep—with her jokes and taunts, her sudden bursts of joy and anger, and her beauty—had more and more power over him, Vasfi loved her madly, more so with every day.

But at the same time, he was assailed by the old doubts. "She doesn't take me seriously," he'd think. "To make sure I know that, she torments me. But why, if I'm nothing to her, does she always make another date before we part, and why does she always turn up?"

This went on all summer.

VASFI HAD been stepping out with a young university student, but he had not seen her once that summer.

He had no time for any woman, any girl, any subject other than Zeynep. It was a torment, the way she kept him at bay. "She's playing games, making a fool of me," he thought. With time, that thought became a fact. Every time they were due to meet, he would tell himself: "This time I'm going to tell her that we won't be seeing each other again." But when the time came for them to part, he'd be desperate to know where and when they'd next be meeting.

They always met far from the neighborhood. Zeynep was still afraid of the neighborhood gossips.

Vasfi began to have suspicions. "Is there another man in her life?" he wondered.

So one day he asked.

"You haven't let me touch you once," he said. "Not even to hold your hand. There must be a reason. Are you in love with another man?"

"Another man?"

"Is it so impossible?"

Zeynep frowned. "*Hoppala*, so now you're getting jealous?"

"I'm not jealous!" Vasfi cried.

"Then what are you trying to say?"

"I'm trying to understand why you're so distant . . ."

With a smile, Zeynep took him by the arm. "I'm a serious girl, that's the thing. If I had a sweetheart, why would I be spending all God's days wandering around these cinemas and pudding shops and pastry shops? If you want us to keep seeing each other, you have to use your brains. In plain Turkish, I'm not one of those girls who fools around."

LATER, WHEN he was in prison, Vasfi would often ask himself if his downfall had been Zeynep's doing. And each time, he'd told himself, "No. "Zeynep was not the one who pushed me over the edge. It was my doing, my fault alone. I'm the guilty party. Not Zeynep. I loved her, but I couldn't get her to love me. I was nothing to her, I had no part whatsoever in her life, but even so, I sacrificed my life for her. Sacrificed everything. For her. I sacrificed it all for Zeynep."

He should have accepted her indifference. This fierce love he'd felt for her had been nothing short of madness. Vasfi was sure of her sincerity: This girl who'd not let him touch so much as her fingertips was worthy of his eternal respect. Despite her vulgarity and her frivolous ways, he believed her to be a serious, straightforward girl. But how desperately he'd longed for this girl to show him some compassion. He'd loved her madly. And she was so very beautiful . . . with her olive skin, smooth as silk, and her narrow waist. Her flushed cheeks, her ruby lips, those large shining eyes, and her irrepressible joy. As lovely and delightful as a cherry branch, he thought. And there was nothing he was not prepared to do to win her love.

He thought about this a great deal while in prison, telling himself over and over that Zeynep had played no part in his undoing. She might have been the reason for his undoing, but in no way had she spurred him on. Yes, Vasfi had been ready to sacrifice anything for her, but she had wanted nothing from him. Even now, Vasfi was not sure why he'd done what he'd done. He still couldn't explain it to himself. Zeynep was not the girl he'd thought she was. He'd created his own image of her. He thought back to the day he found Zeynep in his great-uncle's house, in his aunt Naile's room. The Zeynep he'd seen that day was an entirely different woman, but by then he'd become that woman's toy. He was blind to what he saw that day. He had not wanted to see the truth. Zeynep had been deceiving him, calming him with words he lacked the will to understand.

One Sunday morning when he was still in bed, his mother came in with a brazier. She set it down next to his bed and went over to Vasfi, bending down to give him a kiss.

"Time to wake up, my child. It's ten o'clock."

"All right, dear Mother."

She went down to make his tea, returning a few minutes later with a tray.

As Vasfi picked up his tea, his mother sat beside him.

"My son," she said, "I have a favor to ask of you. Please don't turn me down."

"Why would I do that, dear Mother? Just tell me."

"Today I would like you to visit your aunt Naile."

Vasfi screwed up his face.

"I see you're not very pleased with my request."

"Don't worry, dear Mother. I'll go see Aunt Naile. I'm very fond of her. But . . . my great-uncle will be there, too, and that man gets on my nerves."

His mother smiled. "Now is that any way to speak about your elders? Don't forget—he's your father's uncle."

"My elders! We're not meant to criticize them, but where are they when we need them? Who cares about our elders, Mother? Nuri has every reason under the sun to hate that man."

44

"Nuri is not one to think deeply."

"That's not how I see it."

"Listen, Vasfi. Aunt Naile is in a very bad way. You know, she's already calling you 'the doctor.' The other day she asked me, 'Why has the little doctor not come to see me?'"

"She's right to say that. I've been neglecting her these past weeks."

"Weeks? Would it be more accurate to say months."

"Months?"

"Yes, months. You haven't been to visit for three months now."

Vasfi was shocked. "That's terrible," he said.

Since meeting Zeynep, he'd had no thoughts for anyone but her.

"Aunt Naile is failing," said his mother.

"She's been failing all along," Vasfi replied. "There's no cure for what she has—that's been clear since she was first diagnosed."

"Poor woman. You must go see her, son, it will bring her some comfort."

"Then I shall, dear Mother."

"She already thinks of you as a doctor."

"I need forty more baked loaves before I can call myself a doctor," he said with a smile. "Even so, I'll pay her a visit. I promise."

"You've not thought about her at all, these last months!"

"Are you reproaching me, Mother?"

"No, my son, I am simply telling you the truth."

"Dear Mother, let me just tell you this. I've not been visiting because I don't want to see my great-uncle. He's not a good man, not at all. Nuri is right to hate him."

"Don't hide behind Nuri. That's not right. You hate your uncle just as much as your cousin does."

"I don't hate him. He just drives me around the bend. I don't have the patience to be in the same room with him."

His mother smiled. "Why not?"

"Because he doesn't care about anyone but himself. He thinks he's the only man worth anything in the family. No one is as clever as him, or as quick-thinking. He always has to have the last word."

"But isn't that as it should be? He's our eldest living relative."

"Dear Mother, I beg of you, don't keep saying that. I couldn't care less that he's our eldest living relative. I'm not the one who chose him."

"Vasfi. I don't like your speaking like that."

"I don't like the way that old man looks down on all of us. He's the vilest man in the world."

"I know why you turned against him. What he said about your father upset you very much. That's why you're angry with him."

"You're right, Mother. When he talks about my father, he doesn't mince his words. He gives him no respect. He says—" Vasfi fell suddenly silent.

In a whisper, his mother completed his sentence: "He says your father was nothing but a drunk." Vasfi lowered his head rather than answer. With a bitter smile, his mother continued. "Yes, I know," she said. "It gives him pleasure to speak ill of the dead. He says it all the time."

"He's always saying Father died of drink. If he hadn't drunk so much, he wouldn't have died at such a young age."

"Yes, as I said. He takes pleasure in saying this. But he has another reason for not liking your father, as you know. He asked your father to work in the store."

"Yes, I know. But Father turned him down."

"Your father wanted to finish lycée."

"Last time I visited, Uncle said that my father was destroyed by the devil's books. That he was driven mad by them." Vasfi smiled, before adding, "But in my mind, there's no need to be as ignorant as Uncle to see success in life."

"Oh, my son, you know what old people are like, they talk too much. You must forgive them their little foibles."

"Uncle Şakir is so full of himself," said Vasfi. "He thinks he's the most important man in the world."

By now he'd finished his breakfast. He began to get dressed.

"Mother," he asked, "did my father really drink so much?"

"No, my son. He had a glass or two in the evening, as so many do. He was never a drunk. Don't ever let that thought enter your mind."

Vasfi shrugged. "It doesn't matter. Drunk or not, it's nobody's business but his own. My father has been dead for seventeen years now. It's time for Uncle to stop talking like that."

"You're right, my child."

"Now it's my turn, Mother. I'm standing in for my father. Uncle Şakir has started to pick on me. I should give up on my education and work like everyone else. He's done everything in his power to make this happen."

His mother rose slowly, and in the sweetest voice, she said, "No, my son, you shall continue your education. I'll keep working until you're done."

UNCLE ŞAKIR lived in the same neighborhood. A three-story wooden house. Vasfi knocked on the door. A middle-aged woman opened it. A large stern-looking woman wearing a print dress, a knitted jacket, and a black headscarf.

"What do you want?" she asked through the half-open door. She looked him over, carefully.

"I'm Şakir Efendi's nephew."

"Come in, come in . . ."

Vasfi headed for the stairs. Reaching his aunt's door, he stopped and turned to the woman, who was right behind him.

"May I go in? Perhaps she's sleeping?"

"No, she's awake. Go right in. You're the doctor nephew, aren't you?"

Vasfi smiled. "Not yet," he said. "I'm still in medical school."

"It all leads to the same door. I knew you were coming. Your mother promised Naile Hanım."

She opened the door. "Naile Hanım, the doctor you've been waiting for so impatiently has arrived."

A gentle voice floated out from the room. "Oh Vasfi, is it you? Have you really come?"

"Yes, I have, dear Aunt. I'm here."

He walked inside, only to freeze in place, unable to believe his eyes. There was Zeynep, just two paces away.

But this was an utterly different Zeynep. His Zeynep wore makeup, rings and bracelets, and garish dresses. The Zeynep sitting on the chair just in front of him with her hands on her locked knees was not even wearing lipstick. Only her hair was the same. Her curls fell as always over her shoulders, but she had covered the rest of her hair with a scarf she'd tied under her chin. She was wearing a pale gray dress and, because she'd left her slippers at the door, he could see that her stockings were the same color. She was the picture of deference. No sign of the arrogant, haughty, reckless Zeynep he knew. This one looked shy and modest.

Again he heard Aunt Naile's voice.

"Why are you standing there at the door? Please, come in. Come closer so I can see you."

"I'm coming, Aunt Naile!" He went over to the invalid's bed. His aunt tried to smile. Her bed was wide, with a walnut frame. Her satin quilt was embroidered in yellow and green. A Koran was nestling inside a colored handkerchief that had been pinned to the wall at the head of the bed. And there, amid the bright white sheets, was his emaciated aunt. Vasfi bent down over her.

"It's so good to see you, dear Aunt, I hope you are feeling better."

He kissed her small moist hand. Before he could say another thing, the woman who'd let him into the house saw fit to interrupt him.

"She's not at all well, the poor thing. These last days she's been very tired."

In a shaky voice, his aunt concurred. "It's true, my boy. I'm so very tired. I feel terrible."

"But how can that be, dear Aunt? You look fine to me."

Naile Hanım gave him a sad smile. "I don't think so, dear child. You're just saying that to console me and give me courage."

"Why would I want to give you courage, dear Aunt? You've always had courage. It's just that your illness might last for a long time, and for that reason you must rest. That's all there is to it."

"I feel so tired. There is no cure."

"Please believe me, Aunt. All this will be over soon. And you'll be back to your old self."

"I don't think I shall ever get well."

The large woman standing next to him leaned over and said, "No one should ever give up on hope, until our last moment we must trust in God."

On hearing the woman speak of last moments, the invalid starting trembling, her eyes full of fear. She tried to speak, but the large woman kept talking: "If the time of death has not arrived, God gives even those on the brink of death the strength to live. A good Muslim never fears death. This world has no importance. All that matters is the world to come. A good Muslim must close her eyes and await death with courage."

"Please, sister," begged his aunt. "Be quiet. Let us not speak of these things."

"Why should we not speak of these things, neighbor? Your husband is a devout man. If he heard us, he would be pleased. We must always be prepared for death."

"I know I am close to death," his frail aunt said. "And I am a good Muslim, too, thanks be to God. I am ready for death."

Vasfi bent down to kiss her hand. He was determined to reassure her. "You have many more years to live as a good Muslim, dear Aunt."

The old woman smiled at him, saying nothing.

The door opened. Vasfi turned his head and saw his uncle. Şakir Efendi was tall with bushy white hair. His shoulders broad but stooped. He was holding his set of prayer beads and wearing his customary black velvet cap.

"Well hello, Vasfi."

"Hello, Uncle."

Vasfi went over to the door to kiss his hand. As Şakir Efendi entered the room, Zeynep jumped to her feet.

"So finally," said the old man. "You've remembered your aunt and uncle!"

"I've been very busy lately, Uncle. I'm studying for my exams."

"If you say so. But we all know about universities and young people."

Zeynep was still standing, eyes respectfully downcast. When Şakir Efendi turned his head and saw her, his expression changed.

"Why are you still standing, my girl? Do sit down."

Zeynep looked up with a sweet smile. "Thank you," she said. And sat down.

Şakir Efendi sat on the chair next to her. He wasn't looking at the girl now. With eyes half closed, he began to click his prayer beads. The woman in the black headscarf turned to Zeynep.

"Go downstairs and make some coffee for Şakir Efendi. And for our guest, too, of course."

Zeynep rose at once. "Yes, Mother."

In amazement, Vasfi asked himself, "This is her mother?"

How could this huge, fat, charmless, hard-faced woman be Zeynep's mother? Not once since he'd stepped into the room had Zeynep so much as looked in his direction. But now, as she flitted out of the room, she managed to throw him a glance without the others noticing. And in that moment, there was nothing innocent or bashful in her expression. Once again, she was haughty, naughty, and coy. She smiled at Vasfi, and when he looked back at her in shock, she stuck out her tongue.

When the door was shut, Şakir Efendi turned to Vasfi. "Yesterday, or to be more accurate, last night, I saw you walking into that meyhane on the corner."

"There's nothing surprising about that," said Vasfi. "I go there every night."

Şakir Efendi expressed his displeasure with a grunt and a frown.

"Your father frequented such places in his time. Quite a few of them. And now your mother must work as a day maid in strangers' houses."

Vasfi went a deep red but said nothing.

"You need to find work now," the old man continued, "so that your mother can stop working. It's about time! Long overdue, in fact!"

"No, Uncle. I am continuing with my education."

"Your education!" growled Şakir Efendi. "So you go to these meyhanes to replenish your education?"

"Şakir Efendi, let the child be!" cried his ailing aunt. "Is now the time for such words?"

Then she turned her worried eyes to Vasfi. She was asking Vasfi not to rise to the bait, to let the matter rest. She feared that if the argument continued, Vasfi would stop coming to see her. With this in mind, she'd found the courage to speak up. But Şakir Efendi wasn't having it.

"Naile Hanım. Don't you interfere."

Naile Hanım closed her tired eyes.

Vasfi went over to his aunt's bed, took her hand in his, and in a voice only she could hear, he said, "My dear Aunt. You know how much I love you. Please don't worry. I shall keep coming to see you until you're well again."

"Thank you, my boy. I feel so much better with you at my side." And then, in a lower voice, she added, "I'm as lonely as I am ill, my child."

Vasfi knew just how alone she was. She had lived like a shadow in this house, with this man who thought of no one but himself. She had never known happiness, not for a single day. Never been mistress of her own house. She'd been her husband's slave. Not once during her years of bondage had she smiled. She was a childless woman. She'd given all her love to her husband's two nephews. Loved them as her own.

SUDDENLY THE door opened. Vasfi turned to see Zeynep bringing in a tray. Innocent and bashful once again. Standing before the old man in his chair, she said, "Your coffee, sir."

All at once the wrinkles on Şakir Efendi's face softened. With a broad smile he thanked her. Then Zeynep offered Vasfi the tray. In a delicate voice, she said, "May I offer you a coffee, too?"

"Thank you, yes. You've gone to so much trouble."

This was the first time Vasfi had seen Zeynep inside a house and he found her wondrously sweet. No sign now of that irascible Zeynep who was always talking back to him in all those cinemas and pastry shops. Vasfi worshipped that Zeynep. But it hadn't occurred to him until this moment how lovely it might be to share a life with this new one. Never before had he imagined such a thing. "I want to be with her forever," he thought. "In the same house, always together. I want her to be my wife."

Zeynep passed a coffee to her mother.

"There's only one left," Vasfi noted, with a smile.

"Yes," said Zeynep. "It's yours."

"Where's yours then?"

Here again, her mother broke in. "My daughter would never dream of taking coffee in the presence of her mother and her elders. We keep to the old ways, bless God."

Vasfi smiled. "Drinking coffee in the presence of one's elders is not a sign of disrespect, I would say."

"You can think as you like. But my daughter does not drink coffee in front of her mother, nor does she smoke in front of her father. Say what you will, but we hold to the old customs."

Vasfi kept smiling. He turned to his uncle. "I'm hoping I have permission to drink coffee in your presence."

His uncle muttered a few inaudible words.

In a sweet and calming voice, Zeynep asked, "Is the coffee to your liking, Şakir Efendi?"

A FEW days later, Vasfi paid his aunt another visit. His uncle wasn't there, as he'd hoped. But Zeynep wasn't either.

There was only her mother at his aunt's side.

"You're not alone, dear Aunt."

"No, I'm not," she said. "Şüküre Hanım is a very kind and compassionate neighbor. She never leaves my side."

"We are Muslims," said Şüküre Hanım with a light shrug. "Praise be to God. I do only what every neighbor should do. It's a small thing. What I do, it is my duty to do. We all travel the same road. Today it's me. Tomorrow it will be you. A day always arrives when we need another at our side."

The invalid seemed now to be resigned to her fate. With a wan smile she bowed her head.

"I know I have little time left. And I hope that when I'm gone you won't abandon Şakir Efendi. Please if you could help him. Please could you look after his house. It's fallen to pieces, these last days—"

"God forbid, neighbor. When your time has come, I shall look after Şakir Efendi like my own brother."

Vasfi tried to smile. "What are you saying, Aunt? Stop saying these terrible things. Let's talk about the things you'll do when you get better."

There was a small light in the invalid's eyes. Hope . . .

"As soon as you're out of bed," Vasfi added, "we should take you to the seaside or the countryside, for a change of air."

The invalid smiled, as Şüküre Hanım sucked all joy from the room.

———

VASFI STEPPED outside to smoke a cigarette. On his return Vasfi again found Şüküre Hanım at his aunt's side.

"Your aunt's days are numbered," she said in a grave voice.

Vasfi nodded vaguely, so as not to answer.

"The seizures are coming thick and fast now," the woman continued. "So strong as to pray to be delivered by death."

Again, Vasfi held his tongue.

"The one I truly pity is your uncle," she continued. "He's going to be left alone. Alone, and at his age. By God, when I think of it, my heart aches."

"The one our hearts should ache for is not my uncle. It's my poor aunt. We need to do everything in our power to extend her life." And then, looking straight into Şüküre Hanım's eyes, he added, "I've wanted to say this a few times already, but because we've never been alone, I haven't had the opportunity. You're with my aunt all the time. She has a heart condition. For this reason it's very important not to upset her. You need to be doing the opposite instead. Never talk about illness or death or anything upsetting. Never frighten her. The slightest bit of excitement is dangerous for her."

"We are all Muslims," the woman replied. "If she doesn't know the end is nigh, she will neither repent nor renew her faith. She will die without bearing witness to God."

"If there is a God," Vasfi retorted.

The woman clapped both her hands over her mouth. "Repent, repent!"

But Vasfi had more to say. "When God sees his servant on the verge of death, He pays no heed to what that servant says. He looks at the path he has taken in his life. He considers his deeds. I do not believe that the sins committed over a lifetime will be forgiven, just because forgiveness is sought on the brink of death!"

"But it's God's command!"

"Forgive me," he replied. "Our generation did not study religion. I am not in a position to discuss this matter with you. But I am a medical school student. So I know what my aunt's illness is and what puts her in greater danger."

"In that case," said the woman, "you have my word. If it is dangerous to send her into the next life with faith, I shall not speak to her of martyrdom again. Nor shall I read the Koran when she is suffering."

Vasfi realized that he had offended Zeynep's mother. "Still," he thought, "I cannot allow her to scare my aunt to death. She cannot be allowed to kill my aunt with fear."

He stayed with his aunt for a few more hours, hoping that Zeynep might come.

That day there was no sight of her.

He waited as long as he could, leaving only when he knew his uncle was due to arrive.

Stopping off at the meyhane where he met with Nuri every evening, he found his cousin in his usual place, laughing and drinking rakı with his neighborhood friends.

Vasfi gave him a wave, ordered himself a rakı.

"You look a bit troubled," Nuri said. "What's going on?"

"I'm just back from visiting Aunt Naile."

"Poor Aunt Naile. My mother went to visit her today, and she wasn't at all well."

"Sadly, no she isn't."

"It's that wretched man who's pushed her to death's door."

This Vasfi couldn't accept. No matter how much he hated Uncle Şakir, he wasn't going to stand for this sort of loose talk in public.

"What are you complaining about?" he cried. "Has he poisoned this woman all her life?"

"It's Uncle Şakir who's killing her!" Nuri retorted. "Death will be a deliverance for the poor woman." He stood up, rakı glass in hand. "The one who really should be dying is that mean old man. That would bring peace to us all. The man worships money. He keeps piling it up. Does he think he's going to take it to the next world? The fool has only a few days left."

"What's that to do with us?" Vasfi asked.

"Oh, how polite you are, my son. You like to think money has no importance. But I'm not like you. I give importance to his money. We're his heirs."

"As if!" Vasfi said.

"What are you saying?" Nuri cried. "There are no ifs, ands, or buts! We're entitled to his money. He could have helped us all along, too. Helped us find work. And he has no children. Where's he going to take his money, to the wooden village?"

Nuri had already had a lot to drink. He was talking nonsense. But Vasfi was no longer listening.

He'd jumped to his feet, glass in hand. He'd just seen Zeynep rounding the corner. She was wearing a coat. And a headscarf. Without a glance in Vasfi's direction, and with her head held high, she was heading for Uncle Şakir's house.

With sad eyes, Vasfi watched her go. How sorry he was that he hadn't stayed with his aunt for longer.

A while later, he saw Uncle Şakir. He was heading home, with a handkerchief full of the season's early fruits.

ONE DAY some three months after Aunt Naile's death, Vasfi's mother said, "I have some surprising news for you."

She was smiling, which told Vasfi that this news must be truly out of the ordinary.

"So why is this news so funny, Mother? It takes a lot to make you smile."

"Well, we don't hear about such things every day!"

"What is it then?"

"Uncle Şakir is engaged."

"You must be joking," Vasfi cried, and like his mother, he laughed.

"He's not the first man to marry again after his wife has died, but that's not the funny part."

"What's the funny part?"

"He's marrying one of our neighbors from across the way."

"Yes, I ran into that woman a few times while visiting Aunt Naile. She was also looking after him after Aunt Naile died. He wants someone looking after him, in other words."

His mother was still smiling. "He doesn't want someone looking after him. He wants love!"

Not quite knowing why he suddenly felt so panicked, Vasfi asked, "So who exactly is he marrying?"

"Not Şüküre Hanım. She's a married woman, as you probably know. She's not going to be your new aunt. Your new aunt will be a much younger woman."

"Who?"

"Şüküre Hanım's daughter."

Without taking his eyes from his mother's face, Vasfi mumbled, "Are you joking?"

Mother and son looked at each other for a time in silence, before his mother asked in a sweet voice, "Do you know that girl?"

"Yes!"

His mother was no longer smiling. Slowly Vasfi pulled himself together. "She was sitting with Aunt Naile a few times when I visited. I could also see her from my window."

"Oh, so that's how it was. Uncle Şakir must have lost his head, to be marrying such a young girl."

Vasfi said nothing. He just looked at his mother blankly, unable to take in her words.

"The whole neighborhood is talking about it," his mother now said. "Everyone is making fun of Uncle Şakir, saying he shouldn't have done something so foolish."

Vasfi closed the door to his room and ran to the window. He had to see Zeynep at once. He could not believe what he'd just heard. How could such a thing be possible? Zeynep could not want to marry that old man. He needed to see her, to talk to her. He needed to tell her that this whole foolish thing was wrong. He needed to convince her. Bring her around. The window was open, but there was no sign of Zeynep. He tried calling out to her in a whisper. He couldn't think straight. He was ready to do anything. He hadn't the patience to wait until the next day, when they were due to meet again. After pacing his room a few times, he threw open the door to run downstairs into the street.

"I must speak to her at once . . ."

Still running, he turned the corner into her street. He ran past her house—curtains drawn, windows closed. He continued walking, as far as the next corner. He turned around and passed once more in front of the house. The windows were still closed, the curtains drawn. No sign of Zeynep. He went into the meyhane on the corner and ordered three rakıs, knocked back the last one in a single gulp, and left. He walked again past Zeynep's house. Those curtains were still drawn, windows closed.

"They must not be at home," he thought. "But there's nothing stopping me from waiting until they're back."

He stationed himself beneath a tree, so that he could keep an eye on the street as well as the front of the house. Before long, the front door opened and Zeynep stepped out. She was wearing a black coat and a silk headscarf.

He wanted to jump right out, take her by the arms, and say, "Tell me, tell me now. Is it true what I've heard?" But he didn't dare. He remained planted in place, and when she passed by him, he could see her cheeks were flushed and her eyes burning with rage. Her pressed lips spoke of disgust. Seeing her silent and furious, he could only let her pass. It had calmed him, in any event, just to see her. Zeynep was walking in the same direction as she had before their first encounter. Vasfi followed her, and when they were far enough away from their neighborhood, Zeynep wheeled around.

"Hurry up," she barked. "Come here. What do you want from me? Have you lost your mind? What's come over you?"

He stumbled toward her, as she raged on: "Look at yourself, boy! I hate it when you act like this. I don't like ugly scenes. How many times have I told you. I don't want the neighborhood talking about me. Get that into your head, will you?"

Then she stopped, her eyes filling with terror. For now she was confronted by a Vasfi she'd never met before. He had taken her by the shoulders and was shaking her violently, and in a harsh voice, crying, "Answer me. Tell me. Is this true?"

Zeynep went a deep red, and then she went pale.

"Let go of me," she said in a tiny voice. "What do you want to know? I don't understand," she said, as she wriggled herself free.

"I'm asking you if what I've heard is true."

"What do you mean?"

"Are you engaged to my uncle? Are you going to marry him? I want to know."

Zeynep took one step back and in a tired voice, she murmured, "Yes, it's true."

"Oh, dear God!" He felt all his strength draining from his body. He couldn't even protest. In a faint voice he said, "But this is outrageous, Zeynep. It's impossible. It's not right. You must be lying."

Zeynep leaned forward. "It's true."

"No, no. I don't believe you. You're just saying this to punish me. You're just angry at me because I stood outside your house. You're saying this to upset me, get back at me." He paused, to keep himself from sobbing like a child.

"This is ridiculous," said Zeynep. "Disgusting . . ."

He was desperate to not show her how weak he was. His hands were trembling, he could no longer speak. If he opened his mouth, he'd start crying.

Zeynep looked miserable and exhausted. She just stood there before him, saying nothing. A few minutes passed. Then Vasfi pulled himself together.

"Tell me," he said. "If nothing else, just tell me. Why did you do this? Why?"

"It's not my fault. If I were free, do you think I'd do anything like this? Would I ever want anything to do with that dotard?"

"Who's forcing you to marry him?"

"My mother. Who else would it be? You don't know her. You have no idea what she is capable of. It's all her doing."

"But you're not a child. You're old enough to make your own decisions. No one can force you into something you don't want to do."

She made a face and shrugged. "Go ahead and think that."

"But—"

"There are no buts. This is the way it's going to be. My parents arranged all this. Without even telling me. And listen: We're not Istanbul people. Where we're from, parents can give their daughters to whomever they want."

"I don't believe you."

"Believe me, or don't believe me. I don't care. I'm just telling you how it is. We're old-fashioned people. Daughters can't disobey their parents."

"Nonsense. I don't believe a word you said."

"Don't then. And anyway, what difference does it make if you believe me or not? It's all settled."

"Listen, Zeynep. I know you. And you're not the sort of person who just blindly does everything her parents command. You don't have to marry that old fool just because they tell you to. This is outrageous!"

"Outrageous, is it? Stop exaggerating. What are you so het up about? Of course I'd like to marry someone my own age. This is not the marriage I'd choose, but so what. There is nothing disgusting about your uncle. He's a shining light."

"Now that's a good one ... so he's a shining light! I'll tell you what that shining light is you're seeing. It's his gold! Go on, admit it. You're marrying him for his money."

Zeynep did not answer. Instead she smiled.

With a bitter laugh, Vasfi said, "My uncle is rich, but he's also a miser. You'll never get your hands on his money. You'll never have any money to spend. You saw what life was like for my poor aunt."

"Just listen to you now. Your aunt was a wretched old woman. I'm young. I could be Şakir Efendi's granddaughter. Don't you think for a minute that he'll play the miser with me. You can be sure of that."

Zeynep no longer looked tired and miserable. Now her eyes glittered with contempt.

"I'm not afraid of anything. Your uncle is paying my parents a bride price. A big one, too. He agreed to this. My mother arranged this. She's a smart and resourceful woman. Do you know what she told your uncle? 'Zeynep might be a divorced woman, but she's very young. You have to pay as much as you would for a girl who's never been married.' The old man agreed to all this."

"What are you saying? Were you married before?"

Zeynep burst out laughing. "What a fool you are!" she said. "You always thought I was this naïve little girl. I'm a divorced woman. I have a four-year-old child. If a woman gets divorced and returns to her parents' house, it's not at all like the home she left, she's an outsider now, and every woman wants a house of her own, so if the opportunity turns up, she's not going to play coy for ages and ages. Your uncle wants to marry me, my parents are in favor, and no one's interested in hearing what I think about it."

"Zeynep. I don't want you marrying my uncle."

"Stop talking nonsense."

"I don't want to lose you. Tell your mother everything. Tell her we've known each other for a long time now, and that we're in love. Tell her we are going to make a life together. We must marry at once, Zeynep, and bring this nightmare to an end."

She let out a loud laugh. "You're insane, you are!"

"Zeynep. You know I love you. I'll study hard from now on. Become a doctor. In time I'll be able to offer you a comfortable life. Believe me!"

"My mother would never agree to our marrying. You're still a student."

"So your mother would never agree. Do you ever listen to me? You can do whatever you want."

"That's not true."

"Today's parents don't control their children like they used to do. They have no power over their children, no one needs their permission to marry."

Again, Zeynep's expression changed. Now she was tired and miserable again.

"My child," she murmured. "You have no idea what you're saying. It should have been clear to you from the first day we met. You should have understood my situation from the start. If you had, you would realize how wrong you are to speak to me like this."

"I don't understand what you're trying to say."

"So the idiot doesn't understand. What have you ever understood?" Now she was taunting him. "Tell me now. Did I ever not turn up when I'd said I would? I enjoyed spending time with you. I looked forward to seeing you. So then, what does this tell us? It tells us that you were the one who didn't love me. You never took me seriously. You were just toying with me!"

"Zeynep! How could you even say such a thing—"

Zeynep cut him off: "Let me speak. Perhaps I didn't take your love seriously, or your attention, or—"

Vasfi interrupted her: "Zeynep!"

"So now you're calling me by my name . . . You never got to know me, I'm not like the other girls you know, I'm not looking for fun. I'm a divorced woman with a little son. I'm not the innocent girl you thought I was. I never believed you took me seriously. Took any of it seriously. Why is it that you've never mentioned marriage until today? Why so late? Let me tell you why you are mentioning it now—it's because I am no longer available."

"Please, Zeynep! Don't say that!"

"It's true though. I am no longer available. I'm engaged to another man. To your old decrepit uncle . . . I made my vow and he put this golden ring on my finger. I shall be his wife, Vasfi. Nothing is going to change that."

"Enough!" Vasfi cried in a strangled voice. "This is so grotesque it's funny."

"So what if it is. That doesn't change a thing. I'm still engaged to your uncle."

"For the love of God, don't torture me like this. If I somehow offended you without meaning to, please forgive me. We can put it behind us. I beg you to pull out of this marriage. If you wish, I'll drop out of medical school and get a job, and we can marry right away."

Zeynep was losing her patience.

"I have told you several times to stop putting pressure on me," she said. "It's too late now to discuss any of this. You waited far too long. You should have thought about this before. And mentioned it before. My mother and father have made their arrangements. The old man has advanced five hundred lira to help us prepare the dowry. My mother has already spent half of that preparing for the wedding. We might be poor, but we're honorable people, too. We could kill ourselves trying to repay that debt but still we'd never manage. If we didn't go through with the marriage, it would be outright fraud. Şakir Efendi sent me a bracelet this thick as an engagement present. They say

69

he'll be buying me diamond earrings as a wedding present. He and my mother decided on all this, and it didn't end there. He's putting a thousand lira into an account for us. So you see. Everything's settled. And there's nothing you can do to change it."

When she spoke of money, her eyes began to sparkle.

"Zeynep, why do you give such importance to money?"

Zeynep shrugged impatiently. "Keep your thoughts to yourself. Just know this, Vasfi. I don't owe you any explanations. I'm not your wife and not your mistress either. I never promised you anything, and it's my decision whom I choose to spend my life with."

Instead of answering, Vasfi bowed his head. Yes, Zeynep was right. He was a fool. After a long silence, Zeynep took his hand, as if to make peace.

"Just let it go, Vasfi dear. Just admit it to yourself, you never truly loved me. Our friendship was never serious. But now I'm going to marry this uncle you hate so much, and you don't like the idea of my becoming your aunt. That's all there is to it. Come on now, Vasfi. Don't make either of us miserable for nothing. Let's see a smile on your face. Look at me. No—not like that. Look at me and smile. I'm about to become your aunt. From now on, that's what you're going to call me. Don't you think that's funny? How could you not laugh about it?"

Zeynep laughed. There was nothing false in it. Just joy and happiness. It came right from the heart.

"Stop sulking, Vasfi. We shall always stay friends."

Vasfi did not reply.

"Goodness!" Zeynep said. "It's getting dark already! I left the house without telling anyone when I saw you out there. I must get home at once. Vasfi, promise me not to do what you did this evening, ever again."

"All right, Zeynep. I promise."

"Goodbye, Vasfi dear."

"Are you going already? When will I see you again?"

"Are you crazy or what? From now on, it will be so much easier for us to see each other. We don't have to fix our meetings in advance anyway. In two weeks' time, I'll become your aunt, and you can come to see us whenever you like."

"Hush. Hush! Don't talk like that!"

"Oh for goodness' sake. You're so annoying. Laugh, will you. Whenever I think about becoming your aunt, I can't stop laughing. I never could have imagined it! But here we are. I'm your aunt now. When you come to visit, you'll have to kiss my hand."

"You're making fun of me."

"No, I'm not. We're sharing a joke. Stop seeing only the dark side. Start smiling, like me. We're friends, you and I, and we'll stay friends."

She pulled her hand from his and raced away, leaving him standing on the sidewalk.

"UNCLE ŞAKIR is a new man. Strutting around in fine new clothes—you have to see it to believe it. He goes to the barber every day for a shave. He's even trimmed his mustache!"

Vasfi's mother was laughing as she told him all this over breakfast.

"They're quite a team, that girl and her mother. They've even got Uncle Şakir to buy a radio. A miser like him—who would have guessed? And that's not all. They're even changing the furniture. Poor Aunt Naile! If she bought so much as a broom, he'd be grumbling about it for forty days."

Vasfi managed to appear indifferent to what his mother was telling him, but only with enormous effort.

It was the same whenever he met up with Nuri at the meyhane on the corner. Sacit, the owner's son, was always bringing up Uncle Şakir's wedding just to needle Nuri. Sacit was Nuri's friend from primary school, and Nuri had made no effort to hide his distress about his uncle's marriage. Nuri had always expected to inherit from his childless uncle one day. With this new marriage, that hope was in peril. After a few glasses of rakı, Nuri would begin with his obscene predictions. Aunt Naile had never had a child, but this new aunt was young. She would certainly be giving his uncle a big fat son. For his uncle's age was no impediment. Luckily there were plenty of strapping young men in this neighborhood who could do the job for him. There wasn't going to be a blood test, after all . . . So it would be this baby who inherited his fortune.

Nuri would say these things in a rage while everyone around him laughed along. Vasfi was the only one who didn't laugh. The moment Nuri started speaking, he'd slip out the door with his head bowed. His heart pounding with such rage he could hear it in his ears. Sometimes he would wander the dark streets aimlessly for many hours. For as long as it took to wipe Zeynep and Uncle Şakir from his mind . . .

ONE DAY his mother said, "We're invited to Uncle Şakir's wedding next Thursday."

It was evening. They were eating supper. Vasfi looked up with fury.

"What a travesty!" he shouted. "I'm not going."

His mother gave him a long look, and then, in a calm voice, she said, "We have no right to show our displeasure about this wedding, son. Uncle Şakir has the right to marry whom he pleases. No one can stop him. Furthermore, as I have already told you, he is hardly the first man to remarry after his wife has died. It's true, he should have been marrying a woman his own age, and not a girl this young. But in the end it is for him to decide. It's nothing to do with us." Standing up, she added, "I've sent your suit to the cleaners."

Vasfi could no longer contain himself. "Now that really is the last straw. Why did you do that without telling me?"

Never before had he spoke to his mother so roughly. She stared at him in amazement. In a low voice she asked, "What's come over you?"

"I can do what I want. I'm not a child anymore. If I wanted my suit cleaned, I'd take it to the cleaners myself!" In a softer voice, he added, "I was planning to wear it today."

His mother placed their dishes on a tray, picked it up, and headed to the door.

"There's no need for you to be as angry as Nuri about this marriage. You're starting to act like Nuri."

"Like Nuri?"

"Yes, just like Nuri. It's not right to set your sights on a rich relation's fortune, my son. One day soon you'll be a doctor and everyone will look up to you. A day might come when you're even richer than your uncle."

"But Mother . . ."

She left the room before he could say more. When she returned a few minutes later, she found Vasfi standing at the window. She went to his side.

"My son," she pleaded, "I shall say it again. We have no right to openly oppose your uncle's marriage. How can we not go to the wedding. What would people think? As far as the suit is concerned, I'm sorry I took it to the cleaners without telling you."

Vasfi was sorry, too. He had broken his mother's heart. He fell into her embrace like a hurt child. For a long time he did not move.

"I'm so sorry, Mother dear. I just lost my temper. A friend invited me out. And I'd wanted to wear my new suit."

His mother gave him her usual sweet smile. "I understand, my child."

Vasfi wore his newly cleaned suit to Uncle Şakir's wedding. He would later wear that same suit to court, and again on his release from prison.

He'd felt very uncomfortable in that clean gray suit at the wedding ceremony. It made him look like a little boy, he thought.

There were more than fifty guests at the registry office. Uncle Şakir had invited several business associates and their families. Most of the others in attendance were Zeynep's friends, relations, and neighbors. Vasfi, his mother, and Nuri's mother were the only relations attending on Uncle Şakir's side. Nuri had refused to attend.

All were dressed in their best clothes. The older girls flaunting their finery. The younger girls parading in their gaudy dresses, and the boys wearing bright patterned shirts that spilled down over their long trousers.

In his spotted red tie and bright green trousers, Zeynep's father was a sight to be seen.

Even Vasfi's and Nuri's mothers had dressed for the occasion. They'd cleaned and ironed their faded old coats. Their headscarves were bright with floral prints, and they were both clutching new plastic handbags.

Vasfi's mother was also wearing gloves.

This bothered him, but not wishing to upset her, he'd not tried to talk her out of wearing them.

The most ridiculous people in that wedding salon, though, were the old groom and his young wife. Uncle Şakir with that thick gold watch chain hanging over the vest of his navy blue suit. Instead of his usual cap, a new gray fedora. His flushed face gave a measure of his excitement. The mustache that had once covered his upper lip had been expertly trimmed. The same master barber had managed to cover his bright red bald spot with his few remaining strands of hair. As he moved among the guests, he left behind him the scent of that cheap lotion his barber liked so much. The prayer beads he'd been holding for an eternity were nowhere in sight. He wasn't even narrowing his eyes. He'd picked up this habit after he got rich, just to keep people at a distance. By half closing his eyes and looking drowsy, he could demand respect.

But today Uncle Şakir was wide awake. His eyes were bright and sparkling. He looked ten years younger.

As he approached Zeynep, his face brightened with joy. She was wearing a light blue dress under her black coat. A red-and-yellow floral scarf covered her lovely hair. She was wearing black high heels and blue gloves and holding a bouquet of white flowers. Her makeup was dreadful: Her lovely olive skin was caked with pink powder. Her lipstick was tinged with purple. Whoever had inked up her eyebrows had made a travesty of her face.

She looked ugly now in Vasfi's eyes, but he still loved her. So very much. More than ever before. Because he knew now that he'd lost her. How miserable he felt. Miserable and hopeless and madly jealous.

They took their seats in one of the back rows. At the table in the front, Uncle Şakir and Zeynep sat with the two fat gentlemen who would be their witnesses. In front of them sat the register they would soon be signing. Vasfi was sitting next to his mother, as cold as ice, hands trembling, beads of sweat on his forehead. He was trying to contain himself, but the salon was so quiet that he was sure everyone present could hear his pounding heart grow louder with every second.

THE CEREMONY went on and on. But now Zeynep had picked up the pen to sign the register. At that moment Vasfi lurched forward. What had made him do that? Why such impatience? What was he trying to do? He hadn't the faintest idea. Had he had in mind to pounce on Zeynep and yank her away? Or put his hands around his uncle's throat and throttle him? Perhaps all he'd wanted was to leave this room, rush outside so he could breathe. At just that moment he felt a sweet hand take his and hold it there.

It was his mother's.

After Şakir Efendi had signed the register, the witnesses followed suit. The little wedding official said his piece.

The guests congratulated the newlyweds, after which Zeynep's friends stood up to help her mother pass around the wedding candy. These were packed in decorated boxes. Children swarmed forward, each fighting to get theirs first. Their mothers did their best to restrain them, some quietly, some with slaps, and others with stern looks.

Vasfi and his mother stood to one side with Nuri's mother and a few neighbors who had also loved Aunt Naile very much.

"Poor Aunt Naile," one of these women said. "Her shroud hasn't even faded."

Şakir Efendi stood next to his bride, dabbing the sweat from his neck and forehead with a handkerchief. A hand took hold of Vasfi's arm, as a voice whispered in his ear, "Just look at your uncle. He's drowning in bliss."

It was Nuri. Startled to see him, Vasfi said, "So you're here, are you?" He turned to look at him. "Have you been here all along?"

"No, but I'm here now. I'd decided not to come, but then I changed my mind. After all, this is a spectacle you don't get to see every day. When you go to a ceremony for an old dog who's well past his seventieth birthday, it's usually a funeral, not a wedding. Not everyone is lucky enough to experience something like this."

Sacit, who was standing next to Nuri, began to laugh. But Vasfi was not about to join him. This thing that everyone else found laughable was the worst thing that had ever happened to him. He'd never known such anguish. He warned himself: There was nothing to be gained from angering Nuri. But he couldn't stop himself. He took his cousin by the collar and pushed him to the wall. But Nuri kept shouting, kept trying to tell the world what he thought of this wedding. While Sacit laughed along, and Vasfi stood there, in silence. No smiles. No laughter.

Nuri noticed now how miserable Vasfi was.

"Hey now, what's got into you? You look pretty upset! And now you're not talking. Has the cat bitten off your tongue? You can stop looking so gloomy. Just say goodbye to your uncle's fortune. There's nothing to be done. Except to give up. Is that what's bothering you?"

Vasfi shrugged his shoulders.

"I've said goodbye to my uncle's fortune," Nuri continued. "I don't even think about it. Never in my life have I seen a couple so well matched. They've been blessed now, so let's go—"

Vasfi cut him off. "Enough."

"Give it up, cousin. Our uncle may never see an heir, but our sons will inherit his fortune."

Sacit was still laughing.

"Lower your voice, Nuri. People might hear you."

People definitely could hear him. His voice was very loud. But Vasfi couldn't hear a thing. He was in a trance. His eyes were on Zeynep, who was walking toward the door with her husband, Şakir Efendi.

A young photographer ran up to them, hoping for a souvenir picture.

Uncle Şakir made to refuse him, but Zeynep was already smiling for the camera. Seeing this, Nuri burst out laughing again.

"Oh, my my my. Just look at our groom now. See how he's posing. It wouldn't kill you to laugh with us, you know."

THE TAXIS Şakir Efendi had hired for the occasion were outside waiting for the guests. Vasfi got into one of them with Nuri, Sacit, and two other young men.

When he thought about it now, he couldn't help asking himself, "Is this a nightmare? His uncle's house, that joy, that wedding feast, that spiced pilaf . . ."

The rakı was flowing like water. The laughter grew steadily louder.

How ravishing Zeynep looked in the mesh veil and dress she donned after returning to the house. Her makeup looked softer in lamplight.

The doors to the room where Aunt Naile had died were closed. In the room just opposite, young people were dancing to records. The older guests were drinking rakı around the table they'd set up downstairs. In one corner three Coptic musicians were playing Turkish folk songs. One was a blind violinist. Another was a white-haired woman, and the third was a young man with bushy hair. In the middle of the room were two dancers. Both lithe, slim, and olive-skinned. As they twisted and turned, the sequins on their dresses sparkled. The old woman, who was playing the tambourine sang: *"Oooh, ohhh, ohhh, my dancer . . . are you looking at me, or is that just how it looks to me . . ."*

The guests at the tables were waving their arms to the beat. Everyone was having a very good time, except for Vasfi.

How very often this terrible night had come back to him in nightmares. He'd wake up in a fright, jumping from his bed. Not a wink of sleep for the rest of the night.

He'd done nothing to save himself from his mad passion for Zeynep; instead he'd thrown himself headlong into the tempest. It was his crazed heart that had driven him to ruin.

On the night of the wedding he'd run off into the night without telling his mother and walked the streets of the city like a madman. Returning in the morning, he found his mother getting ready for work. Seeing her son, her eyes brightened. It was clear she'd been very worried. Vasfi thought a great deal about this while in prison. He kept seeing his mother's pale worn face lighting up at the sight of him.

"Is it you, son?" she asked, trying not to show how relieved she was to see him. "You're back at last! I'm so glad." She turned her head to hide her true feelings, before adding: "I was just beginning to get worried."

"I'm sorry, Mother. I felt tired, that's why I left early, to head home, but then I ran into some friends and they wouldn't take no for an answer. But of course I should have realized you'd be worried."

His mother stroked his shoulders. "Go up to your room, son, I'll bring your coffee."

"Don't trouble yourself, dear Mother. I'm going straight to sleep."

"If you say so, my child."

His mother's eyes were full of love and compassion. Entering his room, Vasfi looked at himself in the mirror hanging on the wall and saw why she might be worried about him. He looked distraught and utterly exhausted. Pitiful! Throwing himself onto his bed, he began to howl like a child who'd just been beaten. His mother left the house for work soon afterward.

SEVEN MONTHS had passed since Zeynep had married. Vasfi was still thinking about her day and night. He'd made no effort to see her and had done what he could to avoid running into her by chance, but still she plagued his mind. It was almost as if he treasured the heartache she'd caused him. He felt so small and foolish next to his old uncle. The vile man had taken the woman he loved. How could this have happened? Vasfi had lost all interest in life. He didn't even care about his education. He had no desire to go to class. His mother had toiled and struggled to make it possible for him to study. Had it not been for this, he would have dropped out of medical school. His life no longer held any meaning for him. What sort of future did he have, anyway? As Nuri was always telling him, "You're deluded, Vasfi. Since when can a penniless man like you set up as a doctor? It's not as if you have the funds to buy yourself a shiny new practice once you qualify. Let alone become a famous doctor. You'll always be on the sidelines."

As much as it annoyed him to hear Nuri speak like this, he still went to meet him at the corner meyhane every evening. It was here that he first heard that Zeynep was expecting.

"The old idiot will be over the moon, of course. But the child won't look anything like him. He'll look like Hasan." Hasan was the son of a coffeehouse owner. A good-looking boy, as it happened.

Vasfi went bright red. "Nuri, you must not slander this woman. I forbid you."

Nuri looked at him in amazement. "What's this woman to you?" he asked. "I don't understand. Where's the slander here? I know what I know."

Vasfi slammed his fist down on the counter. "Then keep what you know to yourself!"

He left the meyhane without finishing his drink. Returning to his house, he went straight to his room. He was going out of his mind. He threw himself facedown upon the bed. Nuri's news had turned him inside out. So Zeynep had something going with Hasan. Nuri seemed to know a lot. "And what I know is that I'm still jealous about Zeynep," he told himself. "How can this be?" That night he did not go down to supper. He told his mother he was feeling unwell.

He could not stop himself from going to see Zeynep the next day. He knocked on the door. The daily maid wasn't there, so it was Zeynep who opened it. She was wearing a beautiful dark red dressing gown. Her luxuriant hair fell down to her shoulders. Her lips were scarlet. Her eyes sparkled.

Seeing Vasfi, she said, "So it's you."

"Yes," he mumbled. "It's me."

"At last, someone from the family remembered I exist!"

"I want to talk to you. I have some very important things to tell you."

That pricked up her interest.

"Important things?" she echoed. "In that case, no point just standing there. Come inside."

She stepped back, to make room for him. After closing the door to the street, she led him through another door. Together they walked into a well-heated room. The curtains were half closed. A large calico cat was sleeping on a cushion in the corner. There was a fire burning in the tiled stove.

Zeynep gestured toward a chair.

"Why are you still standing. Sit down, won't you. This house is your house. You count as a child of the family."

Without replying to these unwelcome words, Vasfi fell into a chair. Zeynep kicked off her pink slippers and sat down on the sedir, making herself comfortable among its cushions. On the little table next to the couch was a manicure set. She picked up the scissors and idly set about clipping her nails. It was almost as if she'd forgotten Vasfi was in the room. Until she asked, "Why are you just sitting there? I thought you had things to tell me."

But still Vasfi could not speak. All he could do was stare at her miserably, asking himself why he had come here. Just the sight of her undid him. Here she was, the woman whose joy and cruelty and matchless eyes had occupied his every thought for months. He had to break this awful silence.

"Before you begin, Vasfi, remember that I am no longer the Zeynep you knew. I'm your aunt now. Your great-uncle's—your grandfather's brother's—wife. You must not forget this."

Vasfi waved impatiently. "There's no need for you to talk to me like that."

"I'll talk however I like," Zeynep retorted. "And say whatever comes into my head. It's best to speak openly. When I remind you that I'm your great-uncle's wife—"

"That's enough, Zeynep. I know this. Why do you keep saying the same thing? Ever since the day you became his wife, I have not been able to dislodge this terrible fact from my mind for so much as a second. I think of nothing else."

Zeynep shook her head in annoyance. "This *terrible fact*? What on earth are you trying to say?"

"I'm saying that it is a terrible, terrifying fact. I'm saying it kills me to have no power to change it. I'm saying I am still suffering. That's all . . ."

Vasfi had never imagined he'd find the courage to speak such words.

"This is what you wanted," he continued. "What could I do?"

He closed his eyes, fearing he might cry in Zeynep's presence.

"So this is what you've come here to tell me?" she asked coldly.

Trying his hardest not to sob, the young man said, "No. I have much more important things to tell you."

"So tell me. I'm listening. I'm curious to know what you want to tell me that's so important."

"You're expecting, aren't you?"

Zeynep startled, dropping her nail scissors. She looked at Vasfi in amazement, and then, half smiling, half raging, she cried, "What kind of question is that? Have you lost your mind? . . . Listen, my boy, a respectable wife hides such things as much as she can, even from her own husband. Do you understand? What kind of man are you anyway? It has nothing to do with you, whether I am expecting, or not."

"You're right, it has nothing to do with me, but rumors are circulating. I spoke as I did because I wanted to bring them to your attention."

Zeynep gasped in astonishment. No longer her sarcastic, taunting self. Her eyes were on fire. It was clear that she would stop at nothing to defend herself. She looked like a cornered leopard.

"Why did you stop? Keep talking. Is this what you came to tell me?"

"They're saying the child is not my uncle's," he said hoarsely. "They're saying the child's father is Hasan from the coffeehouse."

"And who is this Hasan? I don't know any Hasan."

In a rage, Vasfi jumped to his feet.

"Liar! We ran into him at the pastry shop. He was sitting at the next table. When we greeted each other, you asked me who he was, and then you told me that he was a handsome boy. The whole time we were there, you couldn't take your eyes off each other!"

He clapped his hands over his eyes, before vaulting across the room to take Zeynep by the shoulders and shake her violently.

"Tell me," he bellowed. "Tell me now. He's the child's father, isn't he?"

Zeynep had turned ghostly pale. As she struggled to escape his grasp, she whispered, "Vasfi, have you gone mad?"

It was true. He'd gone mad. Possessed by a jealousy so powerful as to burn him up inside.

Zeynep might have married, but he'd never given her up. He'd kept loving her, but from a distance, as if she were dead. As if she were beyond his reach, and everyone else's. He'd tried to convince himself that it was Zeynep's mother who'd talked her into this marriage.

That she agreed because she was a divorced woman who wanted a life of peace and comfort, who longed to be the mistress of her own home. She was the daughter of a penniless cook. She'd been dazzled by Uncle Şakir's money. Of course she didn't love him, but she was loyal to him, because appearances notwithstanding, she was a decent and honorable woman. She would remain loyal to her husband to the end. She would be indebted to him for the prosperity he had brought her. She would thank him forever for his generosity.

Nuri lost no opportunity to speak against Zeynep. But this time, Vasfi had chosen to believe him. Because he'd quarreled a few times with this handsome boy named Hasan. Because Zeynep had told Vasfi how handsome she thought he was, many more times than once. Whenever he'd tried to kiss Zeynep and she'd brushed him off, he'd asked himself if she loved someone else. And this was how it had always been, because Zeynep had never once let him kiss her.

His whole body was on fire with jealousy. Was this a painful reminder of the jealousy that had once consumed him? Or had this violent jealousy been burning inside him all along?

As he shook Zeynep, he said the same thing over and over. "You're a liar! Nothing but a liar. Confess that you're his mistress."

Fearful and astonished though she was, Zeynep somehow managed to stand up.

"Let me go," she moaned. "I'm not your wife."

At that moment Vasfi saw his assault for what it was. He let go. They stood there facing each other, close enough to her warm body for Vasfi to catch a whiff of amber and cloves.

"I've gone mad," Vasfi told himself. "I'm certifiable. Even worse . . . I am an idiot, a laughingstock!"

And perhaps Zeynep could tell what he was thinking, because suddenly she changed.

"Now listen. Listen to me. It's only my husband's business what I do or did. Who are you to ask me such questions? I'm a married woman. I can have as many children as I wish! It's my business and no one else's! If there's anything suspicious going on, it's for my husband to be suspicious. Do you understand? No one has the right to judge me."

They were standing so close that they were almost touching, but Zeynep did not take a single step back. For Vasfi, stepping back was an impossibility. He longed to take her hands in his, but he lacked the courage.

"Forgive me, Zeynep," he said miserably.

Seeing that she had nothing more to fear, Zeynep recovered her old pompous tone.

"You're not to call me Zeynep. You're to address me as Aunt."

"Never. Are you crazy?"

"Listen," she said, "I know you hate me and I know why."

"I don't hate you, Zeynep," he moaned. "I am trying to stop loving you. But I can't."

"Aren't you ashamed, to be speaking to your uncle's wife like this? Aren't you ashamed of yourself, for making me angry? I am an honorable woman who is loyal to her husband. Don't think you can scare me with slander and make me bow before you. Stop sniffing around me! You and your people have not even the worth of a stamp in my eyes. I couldn't care less what the neighborhood hags say about me. You're nothings, every last one of you."

His eyes still on Zeynep's flushed cheeks, for they were close enough to touch, Vasfi murmured, "I only came here to tell you how you were being slandered."

"Slander!" Zeynep yelled. "I didn't say it, you did. Yes, it's slander. This is malicious slander. Slander spread by hags and witches who envy me. They're jealous of my youth, my beauty. My happiness and comfort. They're just bursting with jealousy. My husband knows better than they do what kind of woman I am. He knows me so well, he loves me more every day, and every day his respect for me grows, too. Let them go and speak against me to my husband. I'm telling you, Vasfi. Nothing would come of it."

"She's right," Vasfi thought. "I have no doubt that she's a woman of honor." Thinking this soothed his nerves.

Zeynep carried on talking, her fury unabated. "I don't know who's been spreading this gossip, but I am guessing Nuri's mother had a hand in it. The woman has a grudge against me. But is it my fault if I'm young,

90

beautiful, and very, very happy? That witch hates me for being happy and comfortable. I've made an old man happy. The poor soul never had a happy day in his life before now—he didn't even know how to laugh. But now he does. He's a happy man. I'm the one who brought joy into his life, and if he gives me a comfortable life in return, is that too much?"

Vasfi listened in silence.

"What is it that you took from me and cannot give back? Were you so very close to Naile Hanım? I've no time for fine words. When the poor woman was breathing her last, my mother was the only one there. Tell me, where was her family when she needed it?"

Encouraged by Vasfi's silence, Zeynep continued.

"Before your uncle married me, was he sharing his fortune with his family? Did our marriage cause him to cut off an allowance? What makes you think you can march in here and tell me what to do? Listen, I am Şakir Efendi's married wife. If I wish, I can have many children, not just one!"

"Enough, Zeynep!"

"Enough, you say. No, you are going to listen. Since the day I married, you've all been waiting for me to fail. You'd drown me in a spoonful of water if you could. When you see me with a pair of new shoes, or a hat, or a new bracelet, you go mad with envy and start making up stories. I am also from this neighborhood, I never heard anyone say a thing against Şakir Efendi, but ever since he married me, his name is on everyone's lips, everything he does is news. I put on a brooch that my husband has given me, and the witches are up in arms about it. Don't they have anything else to talk about? If my husband is happy with me and gives me presents, it is without a doubt because I am very good to him. He's happy in my company, and why shouldn't he be? I keep a clean and happy house for him. He has a wife who smiles when she sees him, who waits for him at the window every evening. An honest, devoted wife who loves him. Yes, I love this uncle of yours, who is old enough to be my grandfather. Leave me alone."

Zeynep's eyes were bright with fury.

"Do you think I don't know why your family doesn't like me?" Zeynep cried. "Your family hates me. Especially Nuri and his mother. They'd do anything to get rid of me. All they care about is his fortune. If I have children, Nuri won't get any of it. So why did you come here? To hear the truth? The truth you fear? What gives a boy your age the courage to come and ask your aunt—yes, it's true, I'm your aunt, don't you dare try and interrupt me—what makes him think he can come up to his aunt and ask if she's expecting? If I were, and not even my husband knew, who are you to think you can ask?"

She was right—this Vasfi knew. He was feeling very much at fault now.

"I'm sorry, Zeynep," he said in a small voice. "You're right. I did wrong. But I honestly did not want to upset you."

Zeynep continued as if she'd not heard him: "So anyway. No need for me to leave you in suspense. Go and give your family the happy news. I'm not expecting."

"Zeynep, I beg you. Let's just leave it there."

"No. Let's not. On the subject of Hasan. I don't remember ever meeting this boy. If I spoke of him before, it would have been to make you jealous. I loved you, Vasfi..."

Vasfi felt his heart pounding. He felt as much joy in that moment as pain.

"Zeynep..."

Zeynep took hold of Vasfi's arms, digging in her nails as she shook him. "Yes, I loved you," she hissed, her eyes full of hatred. "But what did you do about it? Did you want to marry me? Before your uncle came into the picture, did you ever tell me that you wanted us to marry? Why is it that it only occurred to you after I'd been promised to your uncle? That was the long and the short of it. As you know only too well. You thought that I'd give up your uncle if you proposed to me. And keep your inheritance safe."

"Zeynep! Hush! You have no right to provoke me. You know how madly I loved you, and still do. I love you so very much..."

Vasfi took Zeynep into his arms. She did not resist. She rested her head on Vasfi's shoulder. He kissed her hair.

"My Zeynep. My dearest Zeynep."

Without warning, Zeynep raised her head, threw her arms around him, and drew his lips to hers.

Then just as suddenly, she slipped from his arms and threw herself upon the sedir.

"Go, Vasfi. Leave at once. Don't stay another minute," she begged. "I never want to see you again."

Vasfi walked over to her and bent down, slowly reaching out to her shoulders. They heard a door opening. Zeynep jumped up at once. All panic and excitement erased from her face.

"It must be the maid," she said, in a perfectly calm voice. "Back from the market." In a lower voice, she added, "Stay where you are. Better that she doesn't see us together. Wipe your lips, there's some of my lipstick on them."

She went to the mirror to straighten out her hair, before quickly leaving the room. As he listened to her voice, his heart filled with joy. She was talking to the maid. Then he heard her footsteps returning. The door opened. She stood there looking at him mockingly for a moment, as if it pleased her to see Vasfi sitting motionless just where she'd left him. The young man's eyes were on fire with love and elation. Closing the door, she laughed.

"By God you're a crazy one! No doubt in my mind. Look at you, sitting there like a statue! Not moving a muscle. Come on now. Get going, and don't make any noise. I don't want the maid to see you. Why are you still sitting there? Get up and go."

"Oh Zeynep, I'm so happy!"

"Yes, yes. I know you're crazy. But—"

"Zeynep! Since you love me as I love you—"

The young woman waved her hand in irritation. "Oh for God's sake, Vasfi. Stop this nonsense. I've had enough. We've got to put all this behind us."

"Zeynep! You can't go on living with that old man. You must divorce him at once."

"He's ready to be trussed up, this Vasfi . . . Be careful now. Don't make me do something I'll regret. I lost control of myself, but only for a moment. That's all it was. So let's get you going now. Leave this house and never come back. From this moment on, I'll be honoring my duties and keeping myself under control. I'm not like the other women you know. Stop falling for gossip."

Vasfi did not move, did not speak.

"I'm leaving the room now, and if the maid is still down in the basement, I'll give you a sign. When I do, you must leave at once. Keep the door ajar, so I can see you."

As she left the room, she turned to give Vasfi a sweet smile.

"You know me better than anyone," she said. "Until the end of my life, I'll be your best friend. Go on now. Walk slowly."

HE THOUGHT about that day a great deal when he was in prison. At first the memory would fill his heart with gratitude, but over time, that too was lost to the past. "Why," he wondered, "was she so tender to me that day?

Why did she let me take her into my arms, if only for a moment? Why did she say she loved me? It's clear she didn't love me, so why did she lie to me? This wasn't clear to me then, but that's what I think now. When she hid her face in those pillows, I thought she was crying, but now I know she was smiling. When she heard the key in the door, and she lifted her head, there was not a hint of agitation in her face." No sign of a secret love, or a passion she was struggling to conceal.

No, there'd been no sign on her face of love or sorrow or inner conflict. Not only had she not been crying. She'd been in no way moved. She'd heard the key in the lock, that's all. Certainly, she was afraid of the maid seeing her alone with Vasfi. Above all else, she didn't want any gossip, or any trouble in her life. That was all she cared about. She didn't want to lose her husband. She wanted to stay far from such risks. There'd been nothing else on her mind at that moment.

Vasfi could see this clearly now. What he couldn't understand was why Zeynep had chosen to play this game with him. Surrounded as she was by enemies, perhaps she'd just been looking for a friend. Someone who could defend her as necessary. Or was it that she wanted to become a mother at any cost, so she wouldn't have to share her husband's fortune with any of his relations? Had this been a game for her, or was it proof that she was shallow? Had Nuri been right to say she'd stop at nothing to become a mother? Perhaps she'd needed a friend who'd be willing to sacrifice anything for her.

If she'd been looking for a friend who would defend her at any cost, she'd been phenomenally successful. Sitting on his prison cot, he'd relived that day a thousand times over, and then, exhausted by his memories, he'd devote himself to counting the stains on the wall and the bumps on the floor, the days he'd already spent in prison and the days still left to serve.

MONTHS HAD passed since that day he'd gone to see Zeynep. He'd not found the courage or the opportunity to see her since then. He'd returned to his old ways, dividing his time between the university, the house, and the meyhane on the corner. But he no longer went to the meyhane to meet his friends. He shunned their company to drink in silence. Lost in his unhappy thoughts, he'd become a prisoner of his emotions. But it wasn't just Vasfi for whom Zeynep had become an obsession. Nuri couldn't stop thinking about her either, for she was what stood between him and Uncle Şakir's fortune. Nuri despised the woman with every bone in his body. He would never forgive her for having entered the old fool's life. He'd always assumed that his uncle's fortune would come to him in the end. This had been his consolation throughout a childhood marred by misery and deprivation. With Vasfi and Nuri holding such different views on Zeynep, it was inevitable that this would lead to many altercations. But Vasfi could never have imagined that one of those quarrels would end with Nuri's death and his own undoing.

They'd differed on the question of Zeynep, but they were still good friends. Their friendship mattered more to them than the fact that they were related. They'd played ball together as boys, they'd joined the same sports clubs, spent their days on the same streets, and drunk together at the same counter in the evenings. They loved each other very much, and no one ever imagined that one of their everyday quarrels would go to such extremes. Vasfi had often lost his temper over the jokes Nuri made at Zeynep's expense. He'd often asked him to watch his language. He'd frequently asked him to stop making unseemly remarks. But Nuri had paid no heed to these warnings. Until the end he'd continued with his filthy insinuations. And on that last occasion he'd gone to a new level. This time, he'd been bragging openly about the intrigues he'd set in motion to bring Zeynep down. These could not have been anything other than empty boasts. He hated Zeynep so much that he thought he could say anything against her. He thought it was his right.

When Vasfi walked into the meyhane that night, Nuri was already there, and it was clear that he'd had more than a few rakıs. He was acting the way he always did when he was drunk, spouting loud nonsense. And as always, he began to rail against Zeynep. He couldn't stop himself. And Vasfi couldn't help reacting. He'd feel himself boiling over. Until now he'd always managed to get a grip on himself. Calm his anger. By then, Nuri would have softened his tone. "Please. Don't be angry. I take it back," he'd say. And it would end there. But on that particular night, Vasfi had also had a bit too much to drink. He'd pounded his fist on the counter.

"Enough," he'd said. "Watch your mouth. Keep your nonsense to yourself."

It was a warm, humid spring evening. The south wind had been blowing for three days. They could feel it in their bones. Though there were only three people at the bar, it was heavy with smoke. This, with the rakı fumes and the stink of fried food, made the air almost too thick to breathe.

Nuri raised his head loftily.

"So what have we here?" he said, his voice heavy with threat. "Are you actually trying to stop me saying what I think about that whore?"

"I said shut your mouth!" yelled Vasfi, with the same vehemence.

"Slow down, son," Nuri laughed. "This woman will be getting what's coming to her. Our esteemed uncle will be catching her at it any day now. Do you know who the lucky man is? He happens to be a friend of mine, and he's doing this just to help me. He's setting a trap to open our cuckold uncle's eyes. He needs to understand the true value of the damaged goods he's brought into the family."

"Didn't you hear me tell you to shut up?"

"No, I won't shut up!"

Nuri kept talking. With a terrifying yell he'd never heard rising from his own throat, Vasfi threw himself at Nuri.

"Shut up, you bastard! Shut up!"

He kept screaming as he began to pummel Nuri with his fists. Nuri gave a powerful punch to Vasfi's left eye. This only added to his fury. He lifted a bottle from the counter.

It all happened so fast that it was over by the time Sacit rushed around from the other side of the counter.

He had killed his cousin by battering his head with that bottle. Or so he later decided. The police commissioner was of the same view. By the time they carted him off to the police station, a crowd had gathered outside the little meyhane.

"Dirty bastard!"

"Murderer!"

But by now Vasfi's mind had stopped working. He could barely understand what he had done. Confused and ghostly white, it was all he could do to keep pace with the two policemen at his side.

Arriving in the commissioner's office, he asked for a glass of water.

Instead of water, he was given two hard slaps. He remained still, doing nothing to defend himself, nor did he wish to do so. It was as if he'd lost all self-respect. He slumped down in the chair, his mind blank, his heart numb, cradling his head in his hands.

Then the commissioner interrogated him. Vasfi answered his questions in a level voice. He could no longer remember what he and Nuri had been arguing about. If he did not mention Zeynep's name, it was, perhaps, to keep her from getting mixed up in this story. They had him sign his confession. Then they let a tired, distraught little woman into the room. And oh, what a terrible thing this was. The woman couldn't stop crying. She kept on saying the same thing over and over.

"No! No! This can't be possible!"

Head bowed, Vasfi mumbled, "Dear Mother, it's true."

"No . . . no it's impossible! Impossible!"

Their second meeting was in the head guard's office at Sultanahmet Prison. His mother had done everything in her power to make it happen. The mother who embraced him in this whitewashed room had aged almost overnight. Her hair had gone white. But she was calm and composed. After Vasfi kissed her hand, she placed it on his fevered forehead, as if to release him from the hell inside. For a few moments she held it there.

In a hoarse voice Vasfi murmured, "Forgive me, Mother. If only you knew!"

His mother again threw her arms around him. "My dear child!" she cried. "I know everything! How could I not know what you were suffering . . . However could I not have known?"

Throughout Vasfi's time in prison, Zeynep had served as a symbol of love and desire. She was no longer a woman but a thought, a holy faith. A belief for which all could be sacrificed. He'd made her into a deity, for whom he had been the sacrifice. "Yes," he'd think. "I destroyed my life, my future, everything, but I have no regrets, because I did it all for Zeynep." This thought had consoled him and given him courage.

His love for her took on a mystical aura. He found refuge in it. It offered him solace in his despair. Became a form of worship. And that is how it went on for many long years.

But today it felt as if his heart had died. There was nothing left to hold him to life. Zeynep was now no more than a half-erased image. And his mother was no longer in this world.

THE WEATHER was cool; a light breeze brushed against his burning temples. For hours now, and for the first time in twelve years, he'd been walking the avenues and backstreets of Istanbul.

Climbing hills and walking down others. Sometimes catching a bird's-eye view of the sea between the houses at the end of a street. Or a glimpse of the bridge in the distance. He'd stop to stare at it, as if seeing it for the first time. Ships of all sizes on the Bosphorus. Vasfi watched these, too, as they traversed the straits.

He walked into the silent white courtyards of mosques. Sitting down in the sun his body had not felt for twelve years, he'd watch the pigeons wandering about and listen to the fountains bubbling. And then the fatigue and cowardice of isolation would overtake him. He'd jump up to return to the streets and the noise of taxis and buses. Only in the company of strangers did he find release from the agony of solitude.

After he'd worn himself out, he'd return to his hotel in Karaköy. The moment he walked in, he'd throw himself down on the bed that stank of sweat and mildew, still wearing his clothes. The naked lightbulb hanging from a rope stained black with dust cast the room in a dirty light. On the walls were the sketches and writings left by previous occupants.

Vasfi was afraid to be alone in this room. To blot it out, he'd shut his eyes and imagine the walls of a very different sort of dwelling. A small but clean and charming house with wooden floors painted a bright white. His mother would wash those floors every other day with hot water. Everything in this house was sparkling white and as fragrant as a rose. The sheets as white as snow and fragrant with lavender. White calico curtains. Vases on the windowsills. Every breeze bringing with it the fragrance of fresh fruit and flowers.

Eyes closed, Vasfi saw all this. Despite the white hair on her temples, and her hands reddened from hard work, his mother was still young. It was his mother who had given him this home that was as white as snow. How happy he'd been in there. But this was the mother whose life he'd ruined. He'd been his mother's greatest hope and become her greatest sorrow, and now she was gone.

What was left for Vasfi? He had nothing. This house where he'd spent his childhood and his youth . . . it no longer belonged to them. Other people had been living there since before his mother's death. His mother had sold it in order to support Vasfi. And with it all her furniture, each piece of which she had treasured. But she'd sold it for an amount so small that it didn't cover so much as a kilo of the bread she'd brought to Vasfi in prison.

Vasfi had no friends now. Not a single one. Even Zeynep was gone. She was no more than an old picture lost in the clouds of the past.

Vasfi jumped to his feet and began to pace the room, as he had done only a few weeks earlier in prison. Then he stopped short. "What am I going to do now?" he asked himself. "What is to become of me?" He'd run out of money. He had to find work. Where could he go to ask for work? Who should he ask?

Who would want to work alongside someone with a criminal record?

Vasfi stubbed out his cigarette in the ashtray on the table and rushed from the room.

MODERN BUILDINGS jammed in with the old gray ones, climbing up the sides of Istanbul's seven hills. How sad this city looked to Vasfi, and how crowded. So many roads and sidewalks, buses and trams all crammed together. But nowhere in these crowds and markets and bazaars and clubs and cinemas was a single person who might greet him, ask him how he was, or care to know his troubles. No one knew him here. No one asked after him. Never had he felt so hideously alone than in these swarming multitudes.

It was true: No one greeted him. Not even the man at the hotel reception desk who handed him his key! Vasfi had stopped greeting him, too. He spoke as little as possible, buying cigarettes and ordering coffee in monosyllables. "If this goes on too long," he thought fearfully, "I might forget how to speak." He almost convinced himself that it had already happened. Would he ever again be able to conduct a long conversation? At first this thought had come to him as a joke. But the more he thought about it, the more it seemed to have some basis. He even took to approaching people and asking them how to reach a place he already knew how to find, or had no intention of visiting, just to have the chance to speak.

Just to speak, to prove to himself that he could still do so! Whenever he heard his own voice, he was as happy as if he were listening to a friend.

Since arriving in Istanbul, he'd felt invisible. He could walk through crowds without anyone noticing he was even there. As if he lacked a body. As if there was nothing to see. He was a shadow, a corpse in a coffin. The wall between him and the city was as thick as a sarcophagus.

THE MOMENT Vasfi stepped inside, the receptionist handed him a note.

"Your bill," he said.

"Fine," said Vasfi, slipping it into his pocket. "I'll pay tomorrow."

"No, my friend," said the receptionist. "Everyone here pays in advance. We've let you go four days without paying because you're a good guest, but now your time is up."

"I'll pay tomorrow," I said. "If not tomorrow, then tonight. I don't have any money on me at this moment."

"How are you ever going to have money, when you have no work? Anyone who spends twenty-four hours of the day lying in bed is never going to find work, is he?"

Vasfi went upstairs without answering. He threw himself onto his bed. He buried his head in the pillows. His ears were ringing. He felt feverish. What could he do? He had to find some way out of this. He had to pay his bill, and he had to pay it tonight. When he'd first arrived, they'd told him that he was going to have to pay his bill daily. He'd agreed, and until four days ago he'd done so. But for the past four days, he'd had no money. He'd stopped smoking and he was eating only enough to stay alive. He was hungry. "What to do?" he asked himself. "There's nothing in the want ads. Where to find work?"

He'd looked for work everywhere, and he was fast losing heart. Everywhere he went, he was met with the same words. They wanted recommendations from his last place of employment. He was to get a document from the police headquarters confirming that he was in good standing. But he'd been a student until he'd gone to prison. Where could someone who'd never worked go for a recommendation? The answer was: Nowhere. "I've never worked a day in my life." He couldn't say that, and neither could he say, "I spent the last twelve years in prison." And if they asked why, and he said, "Because I killed a man, that's why"—who could get away with that? If he hid the truth and said he was a student, who would believe him? Fifteen years had passed since he'd entered the university.

With no references, who was going to hire him? Vasfi had given up looking for work and given up on working.

He stood up, opened his suitcase, took out his gray suit, and wrapped it up. Some time later, he left the hotel with the packet under his arm. He hurried across the bridge. It was scorching hot. He climbed Mahmutpaşa Hill, sweat pouring from his face. He walked into the Grand Bazaar. And the first thing he felt was relief at being out of the sun. He passed by the jewelers, heading straight for the flea market. Arriving at the row of shops displaying secondhand suits, he lacked the courage to enter a single one. As he looked around him in confusion, a sickly pale-faced man with a strange fire in his eyes grabbed his arm.

"What's in the package, brother? I'm a buyer. Is it a coat or a suit?"

The man was wearing old, faded trousers that were too short for him. The elbows of his jacket were patched. Vasfi pulled his arm away. "Let go of me," he said harshly. But the man still stuck to him like a tick.

"I'm a buyer. My shop is just over there. Let's go there."

Just then a second man appeared before him. He was wearing white trousers and a rumpled jacket. He pounced on the packet like a hawk.

"Forget this loser," he said. "He's not a buyer. But soon he'll be a howler. I have my own shop. Come back there with me."

"Have you no God?" cried the other one. "Who told you to rob me of my fate?"

"Get away, you maniac. Break your neck and go. I rent my shop. I pay my taxes. This is my fate, not yours."

Vasfi looked at the men in terror. They were like two crows fighting over a cadaver.

He grabbed his package from the man in the white trousers.

"Get away from me!" he yelled. "You can both go to hell."

He began to walk away. As he did so, the air grew heavier. He could barely breathe for the mildew, the stink of tobacco and body odor. The sour smell of old shoes and old underwear.

But once he had sold his suit, he could count himself an old hand.

He paid many more visits to the flea market. He sold all his underwear and all his clothes. Soon it came time to sell his watch. It had been a gift from his mother.

She'd given it to him on the day he'd graduated from lycée.

It felt so terrible to be selling it now for a few pennies.

But he needed the money so much that he couldn't afford not to sell it.

He sold it to a tiny man with thick glasses.

When he learned of Vasfi's address, he looked him up and down in suspicion, so infuriating Vasfi that it was all he could do not to hit the man.

BEFORE HE ran through all his money, he checked out of the hotel. His last months had taught him how hard it was to bear hunger. It was a day in October when he left the hotel for good. The weather was still warm. As always he headed up to Gülhane Park to spend the day. He found himself a bench and sat there until evening. His favorite bench was under a willow tree. He would watch the young couples and the mothers and the children who came to play with their nannies. Before him was the clear blue sea. At the foot of the green hills on the other side was Üsküdar. Magnificent, wondrous Üsküdar, whose windows seemed almost on fire with the setting sun. But Vasfi had no eyes for this enchanting spectacle. In his mind there was room for just one question, which he repeated to himself like a broken record: "What will I do tonight?" What would he do? . . . He knew from before that Istanbul was full of coffeehouses that stayed open all night. But he'd never used them. That night he set out to find one, and he did, in Beyoğlu, in the basement of an old building on one of the lanes leading up to İstiklal. Benches lined the walls. In the middle were tables with four chairs each. It was a large space, but because it was always packed, it was still hard to find a seat. A sly-eyed boy waited on the tables, while his boss kept a sharp watch on the comings and goings. By the second night, Vasfi knew that he had to get there early to find a good spot.

Because it was impossible to sleep at the tables in the center, that first night was torture. It wasn't easy to sleep with your elbows on the table and your head in your hands. As tired as he was, he'd not slept a wink. And how it shamed him, to be sitting in this human quagmire. He looked with terror at the people surrounding him. They stank of alcohol. They were dressed in dirty rags and torn shoes. Their hair had never seen a comb. Their eyes were blank, drowsy, deathlike. What had driven them to this—hunger, exhaustion, alcohol, or hashish? Vasfi had no idea . . . To live among them, sharing their life, was for him the harshest of punishments.

After that first night, he too got used to sleeping there. He spent his days strolling idly through the city, until he could hardly put one foot in front of the other.

The good weather continued until the end of October. After months of scorching heat, it felt like a mild summer. The rain began in November. A cold, steady, dirty drizzle that chilled him to the bone and never stopped. Long walks became impossible. He had to find a place to shelter. He couldn't afford to spend all day in a coffeehouse if he was going to spend his nights in one too. He took to sheltering in the waiting rooms along the ferry docks, under the arches of the Spice Bazaar and the Grand Bazaar, and in the great halls of the Grand Post Office and Sirkeci Station. He was hardly the only desperate soul taking refuge in such places. There were any number of homeless men doing the same thing, and if they stayed too long they got kicked out. It was because he feared attracting that sort of attention that Vasfi changed location frequently. Everyone got kicked out sooner or later, except for a few vagrants who seemed to have special privileges. There was always at least one.

In the Grand Post Office there were two. They would stand for hours in front of a heater, waving their arms as they spoke.

Even from a distance, it was clear they were having a lively conversation.

At the Golden Horn ferry station, there was always a blond man with one leg. On rainy days he sat in the waiting room, and when the sun came out, he sat outside, enjoying special treatment. For the people at that ferry station didn't just let him sit there; they almost spoiled him. They brought him coffee and cigarettes and even stopped to speak to him.

At Sirkeci Station there was that young alcoholic. She wore heavy makeup and a pale green coat. She'd sit on the stairs begging and swearing at anyone who didn't give her money. As soon as she'd collected enough, she'd head for the cafeteria, down a double rakı, and return to her step to relax.

She'd proposition men, and if one so much as glanced at her face, she would chase after them, returning later with a cheese sandwich or a bottle of rakı to take her usual place on the stairs. Even if they tried to kick her out, she wouldn't leave. The police and the stationmasters didn't seem concerned. If she made too much noise, then things would change. But mostly they just mocked her and enjoyed her curses.

He wasn't like these others. He kept his clothes clean.

Ferries would come and go. He'd let them all pass, and then when night began to fall, he would stand up, his shoulders a little hunched, to take a walk through the city. Where was he going, this man whose face called to mind a tired little woman lit up by moonlight? Who could say? The city was teaming with thousands of such miserable wretches. Packing the streets, taking refuge in its every nook and cranny, sleeping rough under its bridges and in its empty lots. No one knew where these lost and lonely souls were headed. Some were in the early stages of decline, others were approaching the end and had lost all hope of deliverance.

"No! No!" he would say to himself. "I can no longer bear this life. I prefer death." But death frightened him too. He didn't want to die. He wanted to find some way out of this, but no matter how he tried, he couldn't find it. It was like standing in a swamp: Each time he tried to extricate himself, he sank deeper into the mud.

SUNLESS DAYS, starless nights. Vasfi had grown accustomed to this and more. He was exhausted, in every way. And soon he'd not have enough even for the all-night coffeehouses. He'd eat nothing during the day, and on his way to the coffeehouse, he'd buy himself a sesame roll which he'd eat with the tea he ordered when he arrived. Hunger had addled his thinking. His mind was fogged. He kept mixing things up.

By now, no doubt, he was just another tramp. He was one of them. The other vagrants all knew him by sight, and because he kept a haughty distance from them, they called him "His Highness the Pasha."

It had been raining without stop for weeks by now. He'd stopped shaving. His clothes were wet and his feet as cold as ice. Vasfi was disgusted by his own appearance. He wandered among the ferry stations under the bridge, sheltering himself from the rain in each one. Clean people shied away from him. They were afraid to be anywhere near him. In the early days, he'd looked at the down-and-outs in the same way. These days, others were steering clear of him! Back then, he'd look at these people and ask himself how anyone could sink so low. Now he felt himself hurtling into that same abyss. He could no longer believe he'd find a way out. He had nothing to hold on to. The only truth for him was misery without end.

He was sitting in his usual coffeehouse one night when the door opened and an aging blonde walked in. He'd seen this drunk here before. Her nickname was Sultan Hanım.

She was wearing a feathered hat and tattered fur coat, with rings on every finger.

Strings of pearls around her neck. Jeweled brooches on her collars.

It was late, and the coffeehouse was quiet. Everyone was half asleep.

The old woman made so much noise when she came in that she woke everyone up.

She was banging chairs and talking in a loud voice as she moved around looking for a place to sit. Finally she found it: the chair across from Vasfi. As she sat down she exclaimed, "So here I am, sitting with the Lord from afar. What a great honor." Angry at his refusal to reply, she gave him a mocking smile. "I seem to have inconvenienced you. I'm so very sorry."

"Not at all," said Vasfi, closing his eyes. "You're very welcome."

"I don't think I am."

"I'm very sorry if I offended you."

The woman smiled. "Well done," she said. "You're doing better tonight, thank God. I'm so glad to find out that you know how to talk. It's important to treat everyone with courtesy. Especially people like me," she added coyly. "Because I'm not just anyone. I'm a pasha's daughter. Yes, yes. I truly am. Why don't you believe me?"

With his eyes still closed, Vasfi said, "What makes you think I don't believe you?"

"No one in your state can have the faintest idea of what a pasha is," she said. "How could it be otherwise?

It sounds like a fairy tale. But it's true. There once were pashas in these lands. The pashas of long ago."

She nodded knowingly as she said these words.

Not wishing to hear any more of her nonsense, Vasfi kept his eyes closed. The woman could see that he wasn't listening, but she could not stop talking.

"My father was not just a pasha. He was a Damat. Damat Pasha! Do you know what that means? You probably think it means son-in-law. But he wasn't just any son-in-law. He was the husband of a sultana! Do you hear?"

When Vasfi didn't answer, she grabbed him by the arm.

"Hey! I'm talking to you. Did you hear what I just said?"

Without opening his eyes, Vasfi bellowed, "Let go of my arm! Why are you telling me all this?"

"I don't know," she said. "Because you don't believe me. And because you don't believe me, you won't listen to me. But I'm telling you the truth. Everything I've said is true. Once upon a time, there was in these lands a sultan named Abdülhamit. You wouldn't know this, to you it sounds like a fairy tale, but it's there in the history books. The sultan married one of his sisters to a pasha, against her will. To make it clear to him that she'd never wanted this marriage, she did not go to her husband on their wedding night. She told him to choose the most beautiful of his concubines and spend the night with her instead. My father countered her insult with his own. He chose my mother and spent the night with her."

The old woman smiled, baring her rotten teeth.

"The next day, the sultana moved my mother from the palace to the mansion of a great pasha. And that was where I was born. After that pasha died, my mother and I moved to a little villa on the Bosphorus. Until the sultan and his family were driven from the country, Sultan Hanım paid my mother an allowance. And then, well, look, I turned into the woman you see."

She smiled again.

"You still don't believe I'm a pasha's daughter, do you?"

Desperate for sleep, he cried, "Shut up! Stop this chatter! Stop bothering everyone!"

Paying Vasfi no heed, the old woman persisted.

"Why don't you believe I'm a pasha's daughter? Why don't you ask how I ended up like this?"

She shook her head, then fell silent, and for a long time she just looked at Vasfi.

"Do you know what loneliness is?" she asked finally. "What it means to be all alone in the world?"

In spite of himself, Vasfi smiled. And suddenly the woman's expression changed. She reached out the hand she'd adorned with fake jewels, murmuring, "You poor child."

This miserable drunk who knew nothing about him, this wretched woman had understood from his smile how low he had sunk. She felt bad for him. For the first time since disaster had overtaken him, a hand had reached out to console him.

With terror he saw what connected him to this alien creature. It was a bond knitted from misery and disaster. "No!" he told himself. "I don't want to be like this woman. I must rescue myself from this nightmare." He slipped his hand away from the woman's.

As he paid his bill, the man at the register asked him where he was going. "Sit back down," he said. "I can go over and kick out that crazy old woman. She comes in here and drives everyone up the wall, and she doesn't even order a glass of tea. You'd think she was sitting in her father's house."

Vasfi reached into his pocket for a coin. "Here," he said. "I'm buying her a tea. Let her stay here as long as the rest of us do."

The man shrugged. "No point in feeling compassion for the likes of her," he grumbled. "She spent all she had on drink. She used to have money, that woman. She had a certain standing. But whatever she has to hand, she spends on wine, not tea."

"Just go easy on her tonight," said Vasfi as he headed for the door.

He went out into the street and with hunched shoulders headed into the rain.

So many dirty, flea-bitten, half-crazy people in his life . . . and now this drunk in her ratty fur coat and her feathered hat who was always spouting nonsense and claimed to be a pasha's daughter, and had, if only for a moment, looked at him with such goodwill and un-derstanding—she couldn't belong to the real world. It couldn't be true.

It was dark outside, and it was raining again.

It felt as if the rain would never stop and the sun would never return.

He walked all day in the rain, and then toward eve-ning took shelter in the Grand Post Office.

His clothes were sopping wet, and he felt as tired as death. Walking inside, he caught sight of the two old tramps. They were warming themselves in front of the radiator as always.

One was wearing a jacket with a starched collar. With his enormously long teeth, long nose with distended nostrils, and triangular face, he looked more horse than human. As for the other—with his long, pointed beard and enormous nose and the jerky way he moved his arms and shoulders, he was the spitting image of Haci-vat, the famous shadow puppet. You could almost see the strings.

Vasfi walked straight over to them. They had, in any event, parked themselves in front of the only radiator in the entry hall that wasn't already surrounded by people in need of warmth.

The man with the eyes of a sad horse was speaking very solemnly, and Vasfi was too close to them not to hear what he was saying.

"The king of Spain at that time was named Alfonso. Alfonso was madly in love with a Frenchwoman. And what a woman. A divine creature, beyond compare. A thing of wonder. I saw her once onstage in Paris. She was dancing. Years later, I ran into her at Monte Carlo. She'd come to the casino every night, and that's where she lost her enormous fortune. I lost all my own money to the tables, too. But what was my tiny fortune next to hers?"

"Divine," murmured the other vaguely.

"Yes, yes, I lost my whole fortune there. So much time has passed since then, but if I could find the fare—if I could fit myself up with a wardrobe worthy of a casino, with fifteen or twenty thousand lira in my pocket—I'd go straight back to Monte Carlo. I'd go there and win back all the money I lost. But why am I even talking like this? I could win millions. Because I have a method now. An infallible method."

The man with the pointy beard had not been listening. But still he said, "Divine . . . Yes, divine. There are women in this world who can be described in no other way. She was that divine! She wasn't simply a woman, she was God's gift. And never shall we see another such gift bestowed on this world. They called her a loose woman. She lived in a magnificent mansion in Şehzadebaşı. If this paragon were alive today, they'd never call her such a thing. She was a fine poet, and a gifted musician, and a brilliant composer. How could a woman of such genius consent to bow to our old customs and shut herself up inside the four walls of that mansion? He wanted her to shine like an invisible sun. But she wished to be in the world, and she had every right. She had the right to live among the nation's greatest intellectuals. And because she did so, in full view of that bigoted era, they cursed her. Even though the poets of the age were her slaves. She even owned her own house."

He continued, "She was the one to greet her guests at the door. Without fear or favor! You could speak of anything with her. Even the viziers would come to her for counsel."

Vasfi listened with amazement to the horse-faced man's answer.

"That era—which was it, I wonder? The French refer to it simply as 'the old days.' In the old days everyone understood everyone, or tried to do so. But are we like that today, I ask? Everyone is indifferent to everyone else. For instance. If I went to court, I could be a very rich man. See the magnificent fortune that others seized from me restored. But I cannot, my dear friend, because I lack the money to go to court. No one will advance me the money I'd need to launch this suit. I beg of you, kind sir, take a good look. Do I not look worthy of trust? I am a highly respectable gentleman. Poverty is nothing to be ashamed of. So here it is, even if I offer to give them half of what we win, they turn their back on me. If only I could sue—"

Here the shadow puppet broke in: "I beg of you, don't talk to me about courts. In those old days—bad days—people were condemned without ever going to court. If they labeled Ülfet a loose woman back then, it was because she was protesting her captivity on behalf of all women; this woman was a freedom fighter, and bigotry was her foe. She paid no attention to what people thought or said. When I knew her, she was Fehmi Pasha's mistress. Yes, that despot. Abdülhamit's right-hand man. That's whose mistress she was. The first time I saw Ülfet was at the theater. When she picked up the hem of her voluminous shawl with her gloved hands, I caught a glimpse of her stylish shoes and her tiny feet. When she jumped from her carriage, she let go of her shawl and lifted up her veil, just a little, to show me her lovely face. Oh, such a thrill ran through me. But she didn't hesitate. She encouraged me with her sweet smile. With that, she left for her latticed box. That same night, I made it my mission to discover this magnificent woman's identity. On hearing that she was none other than Ülfet, I set out at once for her house."

This old man was talking to himself. So Vasfi was amazed to hear the other man's answer.

"Yes, they were lovely, weren't they, the old days. Shawls and veils . . . They shrouded women in such mystery. Please believe me, sir. It wasn't just us. Even in Europe, women were more mysterious back then. Extraordinarily so. I once saw a young queen during a ceremony in Vienna."

"A young queen," said the pointy-bearded shadow puppet. "Yes, Ülfet was a true queen. She ushered me into her mansion like a queen. When I knocked on the door, I announced that I wished to see her. They made me wait for a short time before admitting me to a small sitting room. Then the eunuch who had let me in came back and took me to her room. Yes, sir, just like in a palace . . . A eunuch . . ."

"Palaces," said the other, but his friend kept speaking, his voice rising with excitement.

"She received me in a small pink sitting room. She was wearing an evening dress. Her hair spilled down over her shoulders, unspoiled by any scarf. We spoke about this and that. She understood everything. After a time, she clapped for her servants. In came four concubines, each more beautiful than the last. Not even their footsteps made a noise as they brought in our supper and waited on us hand and foot. After we had finished our food and drink, they departed in silence. We were left alone. And that was when Ülfet took out her oud and began to play it for me. And then to sing. Oh, how she played! How she sang! Her voice will be with me for the rest of my days! She spoke to me of literature. Recited verses by Fuzuli, Baki, Nedim, and even Omar Khayyám. First she delivered the verses in Farsi, and then she translated them for me. Later, when I heard of her death, I wrote an elegy of a thousand lines. But even this was not enough to fully celebrate her virtue and beauty. After that first evening, I visited her twice more. She refused to accept even the tiniest gift from me. One day Fehmi Pasha learned of her betrayal. He forgave her, but he did not forgive me. He charged me with a political crime I'd not committed and banished me to Yemen. By the time I was allowed back in Istanbul, in 1324, Ülfet was no longer. Her passing caused me intolerable agony. I took consolation in drink. They called me an addict, but what else could I do to kill the pain?"

Now the horse-faced man spoke, again following his own line of thought: "After the Great War ended, I found myself in Berlin. They had gambling halls there and believe you me they were all dens of iniquity. After the club and other entertainment venues shut down for the night, these men with upturned collars and hats pulled down over their eyes would sidle up to you muttering, 'Nightclub. Naked dancers. Poker. Baccarat. Cocaine. And...'"

On it went with these two inseparable friends, each one spinning his own story to his heart's content, saying whatever he wished to say. Impossible to hear two old men carrying on monologues like that in the real world. They already looked like ghosts, these two. Ghosts that could only exist in nightmares.

His patience exhausted, Vasfi left the post office at a run, only to stop on the first step of the great staircase. He was too cold already to brave this downpour. He turned around to walk down a wide corridor. Arriving at a stone staircase, he made his way upstairs, very slowly, to the courthouse floor.

Why was he going there? Wasn't this highly imprudent? It was as if his memories were tugging him upward. His mind was so fogged that he could no longer distinguish between his sleepless nights and his days of restless wandering. As he dragged his emaciated frame up the steps, he could almost see the gendarmes lined up on either side of him. He could almost feel the handcuffs on his wrists. Reaching the entrance to the Assize Court at the top of the stairs, he collapsed onto one of the benches. Yes, this was where he had sat, waiting to be called in, time after time. And there, over there, had been the crowd of onlookers, curious to see what a murderer looked like. It had been under their damning gaze that he had felt the full horror of his act. Pale and tearful, undone by his disgrace, he'd thought he might faint. In vain he'd searched the crowd for Zeynep. In the courtroom, too, in front of the judge, he'd carried on searching. He'd hoped she might come because she'd once told him that she loved him. But Zeynep had never come. He'd never seen her again. The courtroom door opened, and an officer called out a name. Vasfi rose like a robot and walked toward the door. He sat down in the public gallery, fixing his eyes on the young man standing in the place of the accused. The sleeves of the prosecutor's robes flew up and down like crows. He watched the man's accusing finger, his raised voice and threatening words.

"You are guilty. You killed this man in cold blood!" His voice so loud it could stop a heart.

"No, no, no . . . I didn't want to kill him. I'm not guilty!"

"You killed him intentionally."

"No, I didn't want to kill him."

"In that case, why did you attack him so savagely? With such fury and violence?"

"I don't know," said the accused hopelessly. "I don't know. I have no memory of what I did."

And now suddenly Vasfi was returned to that fateful day. Now he understood why fury had overtaken him, and why he had attacked Nuri with such violence. When he hit Nuri with that bottle and hurled him to the floor, he had been taking revenge. Against everything: this ghastly competition for his uncle's fortune, this world of intrigue and settling scores, this hateful pursuit of profit. Those were the furies that had driven him to attack Nuri.

Money had bought Zeynep. Money had given his aged uncle power. The thirst for money had corrupted Nuri. That's what Vasfi had been attacking. To free himself at last of all that ugliness, and to hit back at it . . . to savor the joy of attack.

Slowly he rose. At last he could speak. Because he knew what he was going to say. Yes, he could tell these judges and everyone else why he'd done what he'd done! During his own trial, when they'd asked him why he'd killed his friend, he'd had no answer. But now, at last, he did.

He would speak, defend himself, raise his voice to explain all he'd not explained, all he'd been unable to explain. He stood up, deathly pale, standing straight, his arm reaching out to the judge. He was going to defend himself, at last! He was trembling from excitement.

A hand grabbed hold of his arm.

"Hey, my friend. Stop standing there like a phone pole. If you're going to stay, sit down. If you're going to leave, then go."

Vasfi looked around him, bewildered, as if he'd just woken up from a deep sleep and couldn't remember where he was. Then he passed his hand over his forehead. It was wet with sweat.

Swaying like a drunk, he fled.

BY THE time he reached the Kadıköy ferry station, he was out of breath. The rain that had turned into sooty snow and soaked through his clothes he could now feel in his bones. The waiting room was packed. He managed with some difficulty to find himself a place on a bench in a warm corner. There he collapsed.

How long did he stay there? He himself had no idea! He didn't sleep. Couldn't think. Just one word reverberating in his mind: No! No! No! Perhaps he passed his hand over his forehead and swung his head back and forth, as if to express his refusal. But of what?

When he opened his eyes again, the waiting room was almost empty. Just one old man, two children, and a woman in a black beret. She was sitting by the window, staring into the distance, wrapped up in her old coat. When he followed her gaze, he saw that the sooty snow was falling even faster. The young woman was watching it fall. No sign on her face of thought or feeling.

For a time, Vasfi was unable to take his eyes off this woman who looked so sad and lost. The waiting room was quiet, warm, and cheerful. Yes, it was cheerful, because two of the children who lived under the bridge were playing, and their laughter was filling the air.

Vasfi felt his eyelids growing heavy. He felt so very tired, at any moment he might fall asleep. It took all his effort to keep his eyes open. If he fell asleep, the stationmaster would come over and kick him out. He knew this. He'd seen the man kick out others.

Forcing his eyes open, he looked around him. The feeble old man was nearing the radiator, his whole body shaking. He was shaking so much that Vasfi thought he might have a fever. He looked outside, to watch the snowflakes dancing around the streetlamp. And then he thought with horror of the days ahead. Again he looked outside. It was turning into a blizzard. He thought about work. To get work you had to not be a criminal. He would never get a clean bill of health from the police. When he'd gone to the station to ask for a document, he met with a commissioner with very thick eyebrows. "What am I to do?" Vasfi asked him. "I don't have work or money or a roof over my head! How can I live if I can't work? How will I survive? My only hope is death."

Whereupon the commissioner had spoken harshly. "Didn't that thought occur to you before you committed that murder? If you want to keep living, well, that's your right. But just think: Didn't that young man you killed want to keep living, too?"

"I know what I did," Vasfi said. "I did a terrible thing. But I served my sentence, and I'm still alive. I want to keep on living. Is robbery my only option?"

"Do that and see what happens," the commissioner said. And then, suddenly, his voice changed. In a softer tone, he said, "My son, as a human being I understand what you're going through, but as a policeman how can I deny that you are a criminal? Go on now, do what you can. So many like you have found work in the end. May God give you courage."

Had he ever been part of such a scene? Or was what he was now seeing a dream?

The commissioner grew larger and larger, as large finally as a giant, only to vanish. "No, I'm not sleeping!" Vasfi told himself. How could he have been sleeping, sitting here on a bench in the ferry station, surrounded by children's laughter? That woman with the black beret was still sitting there too.

But what was this woman doing now? Why had she taken off her coat? She was wearing a wool dress that revealed all of her body's beautiful curves. She was as slender and tender as a sapling.

"What a beauty!" Vasfi thought. Then he noticed that the woman was leaning over and that she had taken off her shoes and stockings. Her lovely legs were as white as ivory. Now this was beauty that could stop a heart. And those slender ankles, those tiny feet, unmatched by any other woman on earth . . .

He approached her on tiptoes. And then he was standing before her, looking into her mournful eyes, that waxen countenance. Like a pomegranate flower!

Vasfi leaned over. "Is there anything you need?"

"Yes," said the woman. "I need to know what time it is."

"What impertinence," Vasfi thought. "Does she not see what I'm wearing? How would someone in rags like mine would be wearing a watch?" And then, he thought mournfully, "I have no watch, I even sold the watch that my rose of a mother gave me as a gift! Everything can be bought. I needed money to eat, so what else could I do? Why are you asking me for the time? Can't you see what sort of man I am?"

He said none of this. He answered her question differently. "Are you waiting for something? Is that why you asked for the time?"

"Yes," she said. "I am waiting for something. It could be a person, or it could be I'm waiting for something to happen! A person who will never arrive! An event that will never come to pass!"

"How strangely she's speaking," Vasfi thought.

The woman sat down next to Vasfi and lifted her bare feet to the bench. Vasfi was at once reminded of Zeynep, of that time she'd kicked off her slippers and stretched her legs out on the sedir. Maybe this was why his heart was pounding.

Vasfi felt the woman's feet on his right hand, which

was resting on the bench. These tiny feet of hers were as cold as ice.

"Don't let me ask why she took off her shoes and stockings!" Vasfi thought. "She's so cold, her feet are freezing!"

As he was thinking this, the woman suddenly asked, "Could you warm my feet. I'm so very cold!" As he took his foot into her hands, someone shook his shoulders.

It was the stationmaster.

"Hey friend," he said in a stern voice. "What do you think you're doing here? This is a waiting room, not a dormitory!" Vasfi opened his eyes: He'd fallen asleep. The waiting room was empty. The old man, the children, and the woman in the black beret were all gone. Like his fellow tramps, he felt ashamed to have been caught and kicked out. But even more than they, for this was the first time.

"All right, all right," he said in his most deferential voice. "I'm leaving."

The stationmaster looked at him and softened.

"Believe me, brother, this waiting room is not my property. On another night, even tonight, I could have let you stay. But because of this blizzard, the last ferries have been canceled, so we're closing."

Vasfi left without saying a word.

He was shocked to see the whole city covered in snow. Snowflakes were still swirling through the air. He crossed the bridge. At Eminönü, he turned left to head for Sirkeci. He knew he could sit for a few more hours in the station cafeteria, because it stayed open for a long time after the last trains. Tonight the waiting room was deserted. He quickly found a little spot for himself. It was warmer here than usual. This brought Vasfi some peace, he felt more relaxed than he had for a long time. The only thing he didn't like was the strong aroma of meze and rakı coming the cafeteria.

He was hungry. He had no cigarettes, and he longed for a glass of rakı. He should have been able to manage this as well as anyone. He closed his eyes, hoping to sleep for a time before they kicked him out. When he woke up, he was lying on a bench, and someone had draped a heavy coat over him. Vasfi sat up and looked around to see where he was. He was still in the Sirkeci Station waiting room. The big lights had been extinguished but the little ones were burning. He looked at the coat that had warmed him: It was a woman's coat. An old pale green coat. He recognized it at once. It belonged to that drunk they called Miss Sirkeci. When he turned around, he saw he'd not been mistaken. The drunk woman was asleep on the bench next to him, and she looked very cold.

He handed the coat to the woman.

"Were you the one who put that coat over me while I was sleeping?"

"Yes," she said.

"Take your coat, I'm not cold," he said, and growled so harshly that the woman tugged it away from him.

"Filthy bastard!"

Vasfi felt small hearing this justified reproach.

He had, he now felt, sunk lower even than these poor wretched creatures around him. They, at least, had the courage to accept their ruin. Either they embraced their ruin with pride or they endured it with patience. But to his shame, Vasfi had held himself distant from them and shown them no compassion. He felt shame, too, at having failed to accept his fate, and having also failed at preventing himself from falling into their company.

The young woman had put her coat back on. Vasfi continued talking in the stern, aggrieved voice that he himself found so shocking.

"What made you think you could give me your coat? Did I ask you for help? I asked you for nothing. Do you think I need your help? What business is it of yours? Why did you drape your coat over me?"

He was ashamed to be saying these words, but he couldn't control himself.

"Look at this disgrace of a man! This thug dressed as a bandit wants to know why I draped my coat over him. You were shivering from the cold, that's why I put my coat over you. You were shaking like a dog with scabies. I guess it's a sin to pity someone like that. Ungrateful cur."

Vasfi wanted to pounce on the woman, but he managed to contain himself. Paying him no heed, the woman continued.

"I almost froze, thanks to this son of a dog. Never show compassion to vermin like him. When you see them on the sidewalk, dying of hunger, just kick them."

Vasfi's head was spinning madly. He lay down on the bench. "I must be very ill," he thought. Because it frightened him, the prospect of falling ill. No, he wasn't ill. He was hungry. "I'm dying of hunger," he thought.

The drunk woman was still complaining: "What a dog. Instead of thanking me, he curses me. God damn you! If it hadn't been for me, you'd have been thrown out of here a long time ago. When they closed the doors, you were sleeping like a pig. I'm the one who begged those men to let you be. If they did, it was for me, because everyone here respects and loves me."

Like it or not, Vasfi was now at the same level as these people. This he could no longer change. He was one of them. Only these wretches could help him.

He was one of them now. They'd welcomed him into the fold, embraced him as a friend. Vasfi felt himself at the end of the road. Step by step, he was sinking into ruin. Thousands of filthy hands had wrapped themselves around him, their fingers swollen, their nails caked with dirt. Together they were pulling him ever faster into the abyss. No, there was no chance now for deliverance. With every moment, he was sinking deeper. His freedom, lost so long ago, and so recently recovered, had brought him to this sorry state.

He felt like jumping up and running outside, to go from corner to corner, crying, "Emergency! I need help!"

His face in his hands, he began to sob.

He had never been one for tears. Even in prison, he'd hardly cried. He'd cried the day he heard of his mother's death, and again on the night he heard his cellmate Mahmut sing "My Zeynep." That first time from grief, and the second time from love. This time, though, he was crying from despair. This terrified him.

Now the young woman had forgotten her anger. She gazed at him with deep compassion. In a very different voice, she said, "Don't be so upset, my brother. I understand your despair—but who doesn't suffer from despair, who doesn't have troubles? None of us wants to end up like this. Come on, now, get up, let's go to the cafeteria. Let me treat you to a glass of rakı. Wait and see, one glass can warm your heart and banish your despair. Don't shake your head, brother, accept my invitation, I swear to God, my offer is from the heart."

Seeing that Vasfi was not going to accept her offer, she smiled.

"All right then. All right. I won't insist. It's for you to decide. Listen, if it's hashish you want, I can get you that, too. To tell you the truth, it breaks my heart to see you in this sorry state. It won't cost us anything. I know where to go, who to ask, and they won't charge me a penny. I can get you the hashish, and then one day you can buy me a glass of rakı, and we'll be even. Oh, come on now, stop this crying. There's nothing worse in the world than a man crying."

When she saw Vasfi couldn't answer, she shrugged her shoulders. "Life is not easy for the likes of us, but that doesn't mean we have to howl like dogs all the time. Get over it, you. Look, I'm over it. I've given up on all of it." With a drunken laugh, she added, "I sneer at the whole world."

But her laughter didn't last long. Now she too began to cry.

"I've given up on all of it, brother, do you understand?"

Soon they had both run out of tears. Vasfi made an effort to stand up, but the young woman took him by the arm to hold him down. Vasfi did not resist. Instead he lay back down on the bench.

"Stupid man! Is this any time to be proud? Stay where you are, you've found a refuge on a night like this, so thank God, you fool. You're acting like a millionaire. Where did you think you were headed in the middle of this nightmare blizzard? There's nothing left of you. You're no more than a dog with scabies. You stay there, don't move. You won't even go with me to the cafeteria. But I'm going there now, and if I can, I'll bring you something to eat, and something to drink, too. If I can't find rakı I'll bring wine."

Off the woman went. Vasfi was still on the bench. Everywhere he looked, he saw black spots. His mouth was deathly dry. He didn't move a muscle until the woman returned. When she did, after quite a long time, her cheeks were red and her coat was covered with snow. With pride she produced the cheese sandwich and the small bottle of rakı she'd hidden under her coat. She broke the sandwich in two and gave half to Vasfi. Then she brought out an old jam jar from her pocket, poured half the rakı into it, and handed it over.

"Come on now, brother. Take this. There's no need for pride. This is your right. If I hadn't seen you here in such bad shape, I wouldn't have risked stepping outside in this weather. But tonight I got lucky! And on a night like this. Hey come on now. Stop playing games. Eat this. Drink that. I'm telling you, I'm doing this from the heart."

Vasfi was smiling. "Thank you," he said.

He accepted the sandwich and the rakı for he was very hungry.

"Hey brother, we have to get this done fast. Eat fast, drink fast. If the stationmaster sees us, he'll kick us out at once."

Vasfi knew this to be true.

"All right," he said.

He brought the sandwich to his lips, but he had a hard time swallowing. His stomach was churning.

"Drink down that rakı, honey," said the woman. "And hurry."

The next morning it was the young woman who woke him up.

"Come on now. Time to get up. We need to make ourselves scarce."

Standing on the steps outside, he asked himself if it had all been a dream. The young woman had gone off some time before. Though Vasfi had slept well, he felt very tired.

His hands and feet felt heavy. His throat was burning.

He was thirsty and he was cold. It was not yet morning, and the snow was still coming down. He walked toward the bridge through the blizzard. When he got closer, he saw a salep vendor. He went down into the Golden Horn ferry station. At this hour the waiting room was full of workmen, so no one noticed him. He found himself a corner and sat down. Suddenly he heard a voice next to him: "Hello, my friend . . ."

It was the one-legged blond boy who greeted him every time they met. Once again, Vasfi was reminded that these were his people now.

"The nightmare never stops!" thought Vasfi. First the workmen left the waiting room, then the students, then the civil servants. At last the waiting room was empty. Now it was just Vasfi and the one-legged blond boy. No one else in sight. The boy was looking for an opportunity to speak to Vasfi.

After a bit of time had passed, a stationmaster came in.

"Good morning, Mustafa," he said. "How are you?"

"I'm fine, thanks."

"It's very cold today. I'm going to send you over a hot tea."

"Thank you," said the young man. "Thank you."

When the tea was brought over, Mustafa turned to Vasfi and asked, "Would you like to share my tea with me?"

Vasfi turned to him in amazement. "Were you asking me?"

The young man laughed. "Of course I'm asking you, is there anyone else here?"

"In that case, thanks, I will."

"You drink as much as you like, just leave me a little. I don't want too much. I have friends, and my old workmates. They'll treat me to a few more teas during the day. You drink as much of this one as you like. If you don't, you'll break my heart."

Vasfi was too thirsty to turn him down. Taking the tea glass, he said, "Thank you."

With pride in his voice, the other said, "I'm very happy you've accepted it. Enjoy your tea. As you see, everyone likes me here, we used to work together."

"Is that so?"

"Believe it or not, I was one of their best men. I took care of the ropes." He punched his knee. "And then there was an accident, which left me like this. There was no such thing as insurance back then. That all happened later. I didn't get a penny of compensation, so I ended up on the street."

He smiled.

"And that wasn't all. The woman I loved—my fiancée—she left me after the accident."

He bowed his head. "I've lost the will to work."

Vasfi set down his tea glass. He was now at the mercy of others. How had he fallen so low? Why had this happened? During his first years in prison, and even later, he had found consolation in thinking he had sacrificed everything for Zeynep, but who was this Zeynep?

Where was she? Did she perhaps not even exist? Had he conjured her up in his delirium? Had Zeynep ever walked this earth? And had he really sacrificed his life for her? If he had, then why hadn't he gone running to her the moment he was released? Why hadn't he wanted to find her, why had it not even occurred to him that seeing her might save him? If he'd seen her, he might have found the courage to live and the strength to keep on fighting.

Yes, he should have gone straight to her the moment he'd gotten out of prison. This is what he should have done, without delay.

Why had he not understood that, without Zeynep in his life, he'd be destroyed under the weight of the things he had sacrificed for her? To bear all the burdens he'd been obliged to suffer, he needed that mad love.

He'd not gone to her after leaving prison for fear of falling under that love's destructive power. Today he wanted to find that love again. For only that love could make him strong, return him to his former self.

Jumping to his feet, he ran back out into the cold.

For a time he walked with no idea of where he was going. Then he headed straight toward his old neighborhood. He wanted to see Zeynep. Until he saw her, he would be capable of nothing else. Suddenly he was seized by the desire to go to her house, look into her eyes, hear her voice. He wanted to love and desire her again with the old passion. Only then would his ghastly, gruesome life have any meaning.

He could no longer see the falling snow by now. He didn't feel the cold. He didn't even feel tired. He climbed the steep hill to his old neighborhood and stopped before a gray building. This had been his first school. His mother had walked him here every morning, holding his hand.

Then she would embrace him. Waving goodbye at the door, she would smile before turning toward a hard day's work, with joy and a peaceful heart.

HE CONTINUED walking. Here now was the little fountain, sitting as before beneath the giant oak tree. Then he went pale and stopped short, unable to take another step. Under this tree, just in front of this fountain, Nuri had tackled the children who'd been thrashing Vasfi. He done this to protect his cousin. That weedy twelve-year-old had gone up against boys much stronger than him without hesitation. To save Vasfi . . .Vasfi covered his eyes. This was the man he had killed. He'd been the cause of his mother's death too. Now he was dying, too, of despair.

He turned around so as not to pass in front of the fountain, taking a different route to their old house. Reaching their street, he could not believe his eyes. It had changed beyond recognition. In the place of the houses was a five-story apartment building. All the old wooden houses were gone. Modern buildings stood in their place.

Vasfi continued walking; soon he had reached Uncle Şakir's street. To reach his house, he would have to go past the meyhane, but he continued walking, so strong was his desire to see Zeynep. But it turned out that the meyhane was gone. In its place was a seven-story building.

Seeing that Uncle Şakir's house was gone, too, Vasfi turned around and walked into the large radio store that now occupied the ground floor of the building where the meyhane had been. He asked the man behind the till where Şakir Efendi was living now.

"Şakir Efendi?" said the man. "I don't know anyone by that name. He probably doesn't live around here."

Vasfi left the shop and walked for a while, looking around him in the hope of seeing someone he knew. Perhaps one of them would have some information about his uncle. Finding no one he knew, he asked others. No one knew where his uncle was. Hopeless and downhearted, he was just about to turn back when he saw an old man carrying water cans on his shoulders. He was walking with great care, so as not to slip in the snow.

Vasfi recognized this water carrier at once. His name was Asım Ağa. Hope rekindled, he went right over to him. Asım gave him a suspicious look.

"Hello," he said.

Vasfi could see that the old man hadn't recognized him.

"Uncle Asım," he said. "Don't you recognize me?"

"No, my boy," he said. "I don't."

"I'm Vasfi, Şakir Efendi's nephew."

The old man's expression changed. As he stepped back, he murmured, "Vasfi!"

"Yes, I'm Vasfi."

Old Asım gave his shoulder a gentle pat.

"I didn't recognize you right away, my son."

"I'm much changed, Uncle."

"Of course you've changed. So many years have passed."

"Yes, it's been twelve years."

"Time moves fast. And everything changes. You wake up one morning and wonder if you're in a different world. You were still a child when they took you away." He stopped to correct himself. "When you left these parts," he said.

For a few moments they just looked at each other. Then Asım Ağa said, "If you've come to find people you used to know, you'll not find them here. The old houses were torn down and everyone left. A few built themselves shanties here and there, and the others moved on."

Vasfi listened to the old man in silence.

"Come with me, son. Let's go to the coffeehouse and get ourselves something hot to drink. We can speak there."

Vasfi accepted his invitation gladly. He was freezing cold. Soon they were sitting across from each other in a coffeehouse. Asım Ağa ordered two coffees. He offered Vasfi a cigarette and then gave him a long look.

"If you hadn't told me you were Vasfi, I would never have recognized you. You've changed so much. That's not surprising, though."

He paused for a moment to look at Vasfi.

"Well, everything changes, of course," he continued. "Were you able to recognize your old neighborhood?"

"How could I have? I looked for our house and Uncle Şakir's house, but I couldn't find either of them."

"Poor Uncle Şakir! Though he was spared, you could say. At least he didn't live to see his house destroyed. After he died his widow sold the house to a businessman from Adana. He knocked it down and built a four-story apartment building in its place."

"Uncle Şakir died, did he?"

"May he rest in peace. Didn't you know? Poor Şakir Efendi. He was born in that house and when he got rich, he bought it. He always said that he would only leave it when he died."

Vasfi could not stop himself from asking what he wanted most to know.

"What's his wife doing now? Where does she live?"

"I have no idea, my son. I think she moved somewhere near Aksaray with her new husband."

"Is that so?"

"Zeynep married a man who'd been working alongside her husband. He kept Şakir Efendi's books and managed his workers. In his last days, the old man was so frail he couldn't leave his bed. Zeynep took charge of the business. Her mother took care of Şakir Efendi. Zeynep was a canny one, to tell the truth. She took good care of the business. And cunning, too. To make sure that none of the money passed to you and yours, Şakir Efendi put all his business interests in his wife's name while he was still in good health. Or so she claimed. When her husband was still in good health, they were saying that she loved that boy. As soon as she was widowed, she married him. She was not the sort of woman to love just anyone. She chose this man because he was already involved in the business and doing a good job of it. Zeynep needed an assistant. She didn't leave it to him to run things, though. She was in charge."

Vasfi had stopped listening by now. The only thing he knew was that he'd never see Zeynep again.

"Everyone had something to say about Zeynep," Asım Ağa continued. "They said that she took up with this boy from the moment her husband was bedbound. They say she even brought him into the house. I don't really believe that, but in his last days, she was not looking after her husband at all. Even so. At Şakir Efendi's funeral she deported herself well, had the prayers said on the fortieth day, in the mosque, no less, did not skimp on the sweets or the rose water, did everything by the book—"

Vasfi interrupted him: "So no one ever sees her now?"

"Quite the contrary! Whoever wants to see her can walk right into the store. She's there every day."

144

The old man put his coffee cup down on the table.

"You might want to go see her. But remember this. They say she is not at all generous these days. She's very tight with her money. I don't think she'll help you. After the old man died, she didn't even reach out to Nuri's mother. After taking the whole fortune away from your family, she could have shown a little mercy."

Vasfi stood up.

"Are you off, my son?"

"Yes, Uncle Asım, and thank you so much for the coffee." Suddenly Asim took Vasfi's hand.

"Have you been out of prison long?"

"It's been a few months."

"What work are you doing?"

"I have no work."

Asım reached into his pocket and took out some money. He offered Vasfi a lira.

"Take this, my son. You can pay me back when you get work. There's no rush. Please, my boy. My child. Take it. You can pay me back." Vasfi knew that he'd never be able to pay him back, but Asım probably knew this too. He called it a loan so as not to upset him. Vasfi lacked the strength to turn down the offer. He'd lost that sort of courage we call dignity. He was shivering from the cold, but he kept on walking.

He was going to see Zeynep. Even if only from a distance, he was going to see her.

When he got to the bridge, the wind had grown stronger, and the snowstorm, too. He was deathly tired, but he was going to see Zeynep. He had now reached the central market. Nothing had changed about this place since he was a child. Same counters, same shops, same shoreline. Even the people looked the same. But today there were no crowds, no motor launches filling and emptying.

The shore and the market were almost deserted. He turned into the alley where his uncle's store had been, and there it was, right before his eyes. He ran toward it, passing a man who was draping sacks over the fruit displayed outside. Inside a neighboring shop, a man with a black skullcap and a rounded beard was ensconced in an easy chair smoking a narghile. And now he saw the neon sign in his uncle's shopwindow:

Zeynep Altınelma
WHOLESALE FRUIT

Over and over he read out her name. He'd come here knowing that she had taken over his uncle's business, but still this sign shocked him, made him want to laugh. He could not connect it with Zeynep. He couldn't imagine her flame-like body in this market.

Vasfi moved a little closer and then he stopped. What to do?

Was he going to go inside and ask for her? How could he let her see him in the clothes he was now wearing? Did he have the courage to do that? How would Zeynep react? Wasn't it better to just stay where he was and look into the store?

The lights were on inside the shop, and any minute Zeynep could appear on the stairs that led down to the shop's office. Once again, he would see her standing there, as comely as the branch of a cherry tree. Her face that had no equal, her slim body, those black eyes beyond compare . . .

And when he saw her, a miracle would unfold. Vasfi would reclaim his soul. Once again, he would find joy in life. His heart would fill with peace. He would be strong enough again to carry any burden.

He stood there in front of the display case for a long time, looking inside. He had no idea how long, but time was passing and still he could see no one inside. "Perhaps Zeynep and her husband are on the upper floor," he thought. He didn't even consider leaving. He knew full well that if he left without seeing her, he would never see her again.

A porter with a large load on his back opened the store door and rang the bell. In great excitement, Vasfi saw a pair of feet coming down the stairs. But then, looking closer, he saw they were wearing men's shoes. "It must be her husband coming down," he thought. But no, above the shoes, he saw a woman's legs. After that came the shape of a woman, a huge fat woman wearing a man's coat, with a large shawl draped over her head.

"This must be Zeynep's mother," he thought. Now the woman was standing in the middle of the store. She had a cigarette hanging out of her mouth. Her hands were in her pockets. The porter had left his load on the side.

Vasfi could see from their gestures that the woman and the porter were having a conversation. The porter then opened the door to leave. Turning wearily back to face the woman, he said, "Zeynep Hanım, everyone knows what a miser you are. I'm done dealing with you."

The woman chased after him. So fast and furiously that her shawl slipped off her head, allowing Vasfi to look in horror at the woman who had once been Zeynep. She had changed beyond all recognition. There was no relation between the old Zeynep and this one. How could this obese, disgusting, sharp-eyed, round-faced, gold-toothed woman be Zeynep? The woman had planted her huge feet on the floor. Her body no different than a sack of meat. What a shock it was to look at her. But when she spoke to the porter, the scene got even worse.

"I'm not a fool!" she roared. Her voice was rough and hoarse. "No one's walking me into a trap," she raged. "Do you understand? No one's stealing a penny from me, do you hear?"

Vasfi just stood there. "Dear God, can it be true?" he murmured.

Zeynep had not noticed him. She was already plodding back upstairs.

He stood there for a few more minutes. "This must be a nightmare," he thought. A nightmare he might never escape from. His Zeynep—the incomparable Zeynep of his youth—no longer existed. Zeynep the fruit wholesaler had killed her. But had she really? Was he perhaps mistaken? Wasn't this woman the same Zeynep he'd loved so madly? All she'd done was to hide her true nature. Vasfi now realized that he'd been in love with a mask. The mask had been beautiful beyond compare, but behind that mask had been this monstrous woman, in pitiful pursuit of petty profit. She didn't even dream of becoming rich and making a better, brighter life for herself. She didn't want money to spend. She just wanted to hoard it.

Had Vasfi sacrificed his entire life for this woman who could barely get her heavy body up the stairs? Didn't this terrifying Zeynep represent his own Zeynep's soul? This Zeynep who had struggled to get her bulky body up the stairs—she had done everything in her power to get to where she was. To think what she had done to get her hands on this fortune, and to take charge of her own body . . . yes, every ugly thing she'd done had been to fill her mouth with golden teeth, exchange her smiles for sullen pouts, and squeeze her fat feet into men's shoes. All to be rich. All so that she could hang that sign over her store:

Zeynep Altınelma
WHOLESALE FRUIT

He could no longer bear to look at it. He left the central market as fast as his feet could take him.

IT WAS still snowing. Night had fallen, and the snow-flakes swirling around the streetlamps glowed like stars.

He stayed until late drinking wine at a filthy mey-hane and then made his way to the all-night coffeehouse. He found himself an empty table. He ordered a tea, and as soon as he'd finished it, he put his elbows on the table and cradled his throbbing head in his hands, as if he feared he might fall. He had run through the last of his energy. He could no longer hold up his head.

He wasn't asleep, but he wasn't awake either. He could see shadows coming and going, mouths snoring or cursing. It was warm inside the coffeehouse, but Vasfi was still shaking and shivering inside his wet clothes.

His mind was empty—not a thought, not an image. "Oh, if only I could sleep," he kept saying as he stroked his temples with anxious fingers. "I can't sleep, I can't think, there is nothing left for me in this world."

But he gathered together whatever will he had left. He wanted to conjure up the Zeynep he'd once known. The Zeynep he'd loved so madly, the woman for whom he'd sacrificed his life. He'd buried all his memories of her, along with his other memories. It was so very hard to remember how she'd looked.

But he kept on trying, and at last he was able to con-jure up the old Zeynep, her eyes shining with joy. That enchanted beautiful woman, those eyes that sparkled like flames, that taunting body—he could see them before him.

Vasfi squeezed his eyes shut, for fear of losing this vision if he opened them. He feared this like death. He could not lose this vision. Seeing it, he could say, "She was worth sacrificing my life for." Unless . . . but he was happy, so happy to be with her once again. His vision of the old Zeynep blotted out the image of the new Zeynep. Zeynep the nightmare.

Zeynep was sitting on a swing, gently swaying back and forth. Then she put her feet on the ground. Why? To push herself off! Higher and higher she swung. As he did, too, on the swing next to hers. And as they went up and down, something terrible happened. With every descent, Zeynep changed. Her expression, her everything. The faster she swung, the faster the transformation. The new Zeynep's treacherous grimace left no room for the old Zeynep's joyous smile. This was the worst thing in the world. He didn't want to lose that old Zeynep. Either he had to jump off his swing and bring hers to a stop, or he had to open his eyes and banish this vision. But he could do neither. He'd fallen asleep. He knew he was asleep and having a nightmare. He wanted to move his arms and legs to wake up, but his whole body felt as heavy as lead. He could not move so much as a finger. He was moaning, hopelessly. The old Zeynep was gone. In her place was Zeynep the fruit wholesaler. Zeynep Altınelma.

"What's wrong? Can I help you?"

He felt a hand on his shoulder. He opened his eyes and looked at it. This was a woman's hand. His eyes moved up to her wrist, and then her arm. When he reached her face, he paused, because he knew this face. It was the woman with the black beret. She was sitting across the table from him. She was wearing an old green wool blouse. Her eyes were green too. So green that even in this filthy airless coffeehouse, they still reminded him of spring.

How shocked he was to see her here. What a beautiful voice she had. If only all women in this world had voices like hers.

It reminded him of his mother. Of all mothers.

All women must sound like this, all sisters, lovers, and fiancées . . . How grateful he felt, that she had addressed him in such a sweet voice. He'd always loved voices like hers. How happy he'd felt, when his mother had spoken to him in this voice. How he'd longed for Zeynep to speak to him like this.

Was this woman a vision? A dream? Whatever she was, real or imagined, she was sitting right across from him. She was looking at him, pale and sad and deeply caring.

He was unable to answer her question.

"So you're here, too," he murmured.

Wearily the woman nodded. "Yes, I'm here too."

"Why are we here with these people? What are we looking for?"

"Somewhere to shelter from the cold . . ."

For a time they looked at each other in silence, and then the woman said, "Happiness is finding a warm place to sit."

Vasfi smiled. "Happiness."

"Yes, it might be a small thing, but to find a warm place to sit is still happiness."

Vasfi screwed up his face.

"Happiness. I don't even want to hear this word. It's a word that holds no meaning. We should take it out of the dictionary, so that people stop chasing empty dreams."

"So it doesn't exist, you say? Do you really not believe in happiness?"

"Is this even a question? Are you that naïve? Are you telling me that you actually believe in happiness?"

"Is that even a question?" she said, echoing his own. "Of course I believe in it. How could I not. Haven't we all felt it? Is there a heart in this world that does not remember it? No, my dear. I know it exists. I know it's real."

"Those who believe in happiness are deceiving themselves. We believe in it because we wish it to be so."

"That's not true. Happiness exists. We must not cancel it out. Like it or not, it exists."

Vasfi curled his lips. "Tell me where it is, then, so I can see it too."

The young woman looked at him with a sad smile. "I don't know where it is," she said, "but I know that somewhere there must be happiness waiting for you, and for me, and for all who live on this earth."

"Do you really believe that?"

"Why shouldn't I? I'm as sure of it as I'm sure of sunlight. It lives in every grain of wheat, every human heart. In all we do, at work and at rest. And once we humans have seized a speck of it, we think we have found it all. But then we come to understand our mistake. Happiness is in life itself. It cannot be extracted from life, for happiness is what makes life possible. It is what brings all of life into harmony. That is what we should believe in—the harmony of life. Happiness cannot be owned. If you are not happy, I cannot be happy. In a world where others are not happy, no one can be happy."

She gave Vasfi a mournful look. "You're asking me where happiness is. How would I know. If I knew, I'd be happy too. You can see with your eyes that this is not the case."

"Then please continue looking for it, since you're so sure it exists."

The woman looked at Vasfi with bright eyes. Then, in a faint voice, she said, "You say you don't believe in happiness. Why then were you crying?"

"I was crying?"

"Yes, you were crying. That's why I asked you what was wrong. And anyway, you're still crying!"

Amazed, Vasfi asked, "Am I crying?"

He put his hand on his eyes, then his face, and only then did he understand that he had been crying furiously.

"No one cries from happiness," he said.

"People cry when they know that happiness exists. Once they cease to believe this, they stop crying."

The young woman covered her eyes with her hands. "Maybe she's crying," Vasfi thought. "Yes, she's crying like me, and perhaps she's had nothing to eat . . . and she still believes in happiness. Happiness means nothing. I'm nothing more than a tired man who's had enough of humankind. What I need is not happiness, just a chance to rest. I'm so tired."

He was thinking of a comfortable bed; snowy white, with sheets smelling of lavender. Smiling to himself, he thought, "Perhaps a bed like that is part of the peace she was talking about. Oh yes, what joy it would bring me if, after a good bath, I could sleep naked between those sheets."

Pure clear water, endlessly flowing, and foaming soap, snowy white sheets, as beautiful as roses, and the bed, the air, so fragrant with lavender . . .

Once upon a time, Vasfi had had a bed like this, but it was no longer his. It was his mother who had given him this bed. She had been the one to prepare it for her son. Only a loving woman could give a person this comfort, this peace. A woman who served you like a slave, never disturbing you, never making a noise, but at all times, compassionate: a mother.

As Vasfi thought all this, he looked around him. The young woman was still sitting across from him. She'd removed her hands from her face and raised her head. She was very pale, even her green eyes had lost some of their shine. It was as if she'd utterly forgotten that Vasfi was facing her.

Vasfi closed his eyes again, to go back to sleep. He'd been able to pay for a glass of tea tonight. He needed to make good use of this opportunity. He wanted to sleep as much as he could. Tomorrow he might not be able to afford a tea.

He rested his head between his arms.

When he opened his eyes again, the young woman was no longer at his table. Vasfi had not heard her leave. She'd come like a quiet shadow and left in the same way. Vasfi stood up, went over to the cashier and paid his bill.

"Goodbye," he said.

"Go on then," said the cashier. "May God grant you a worthy fate."

"I care about fate just as little as I care about happiness!" Vasfi thought. Then he remembered the woman in the black beret, wondering why he hadn't heard her leave the table. It was just like his dream, when she had flown to him on the tiptoes of her frozen bare feet. And now she had vanished in the same way. The sidewalks were covered in snow. The young woman's feet would freeze. He longed to find her and warm her feet in his hands. Who could know what street or sidewalk she was shivering on now. That poor foolish woman. How could anyone in her condition speak of happiness? How ridiculous. It was almost impolite.

The first trams of the morning were running in Beyoğlu. Full of men who knew where they were going, and what they would do when they got there. They all had purpose, while Vasfi had none. There was nothing for him but the prospect of dragging his wretched life and useless body through the wind and the cold. Perhaps it was happiness to have a job, to work, Vasfi thought. Or as the woman with the black beret had put it—a part of happiness.

That sort of happiness would never come to him, as he had no chance to work! He was free now. No gendarmes guarding him. No handcuffs on his wrists. Yes, he was free! He could eat and sleep where he liked. No one could stop him. He was free. Or rather, he was out of prison. But he was still a prisoner of a helpless life, of obstacles he'd been unable to overcome. If Vasfi was free, then freedom meant being free to choose to die of hunger and fatigue. "No," he told himself. "This can't be freedom. There must be some better, more concise definition. Freedom isn't freedom unless it offers the chance to live with dignity. It should be more than a word in the dictionary. Only if our basic needs are met can we live in harmony with those around us, only then can we know happiness."

Now he was free only to die of hunger. "I wonder," he asked himself, "if the worst moment of my life was when they first put me in handcuffs. Or was it the moment at the prison door, when I spread my wings and flew away? The moment this strange freedom was granted . . . I don't care about freedom any more than I care about happiness," he thought.

Reaching the bridge, he took the stairs down to the Kadıköy ferry station. He looked inside to see if the woman in the black beret was there. But she wasn't.

Where could she be at this early hour? Vasfi climbed the stairs back up to the bridge. It was no longer snowing, but the wind was as cold as ice. The sea was rough. In this semidarkness, the crests of the waves looked like thousands of little ships.

Vasfi reached into his pockets. He pulled out a pack of cigarettes. He'd bought these with the money Asım Ağa had given him. He took out a cigarette for himself. At Eminönü Square he found a pack of vagrant children gathered around a fire they'd made with papers they'd found in rubbish bins. Vasfi joined them to light his cigarette. The smallest of them jumped up and offered him a piece of paper.

"Take it, brother. Light your cigarette with this."

"Thank you, my child."

"If you gave me a cigarette instead of thanking me, that would be better."

"What use would you have for a cigarette?"

"What kind of question is that, brother? What are cigarettes for? I'm going to smoke it, of course!"

"Do children your age really smoke?"

"Children my age? Listen, I've been smoking for years already."

"You don't say!"

Shrugging his shoulders, Vasfi began to walk away, only to have the little creature tug at his arm.

"Give me a cigarette, brother!" With a smile, he continued, "And when I light it, it will warm up the tip of my nose!"

Returning the boy's smile, Vasfi handed him a cigarette.

THE WAITING room at Sirkeci Station was warm, and there he found the woman in the green coat. She was holding a little hand mirror and washing her face with a piece of cloth. Seeing Vasfi, she asked, "How's your mood today, brother?"

Vasfi just shrugged, saying nothing.

"Okay then. Understood. Tell me, though. Has it stopped snowing?"

"Yes, it has."

Vasfi went over to the radiator. Now the woman took off one of her shoes to conduct a thorough examination of its sole. Between gritted teeth, she murmured, "The worst thing is wandering around in the snow in these things. These soles are full of holes."

Then she put her shoe back on and returned to her ablutions. Some time later the cafeteria waiter came in with a tray laden with tea glasses. When the girl saw him, she said, "Give me a tea."

"Give me ten kurush," said the waiter, "and I will."

"Ten kurush? Hey, are you crazy? What's this guy on? What upstanding citizen has ten kurush to spend at this time of the morning? I can pay you this evening, of course."

The waiter shrugged. "The boss said nothing on credit. Not even five kurush! That's what he said."

"Hey darling. I'm not just anyone. You can tell him it's me."

"Hey, don't you know you rubbed him the wrong way? He told me not to give anything for free to you in particular."

"The dog! No, that pimp you call your boss is not just a dog. He's the son of a dog! Hey now, I spend all the money I have at his counter, and the bastard still won't give me a tea on credit? Now that's what I call stupid. That man's a blockhead."

"Just shut up!" cried the waiter as he headed for the door.

A tiny woman in the corner called after him, "Give the lady a tea, and another for me. And bring us both sesame rolls!"

"God bless you, dear Auntie!" cried the woman in the green coat. "So there, that's what we call a human being. But haven't I been lucky today! A good start to the day, I say! The best!"

Vasfi had huddled up in a corner and was beginning to doze off. The woman in the green coat kept talking as she drank her tea and ate her sesame roll: "Oh, how good it feels to put something warm in my stomach before I head out into the snow!"

She fell silent for a moment, before adding: "It's a good thing you're here this morning, but if it isn't too rude to ask—what brings you here at this hour, Madam Auntie? Clearly you aren't one of us."

"I was waiting for someone coming in from Yeşilköy, but he never arrived. He promised to come in on the first train. The storm did a lot of damage to my garden, and he was going to fix things."

"If I had a house like you do, dear Auntie, I'd never leave it in this weather for nonsense like that!"

Vasfi wasn't fully asleep. He could hear some of what they were saying, but he kept his eyes closed. Coming in he'd not noticed anyone other than the woman in the green coat. She had put down her tea glass now and was getting ready to go. But now she pointed at Vasfi.

"Listen, dear Auntie. If this man you're waiting for doesn't come, this boy here could do a fine job for you. God be my witness, he's a very good boy. Don't judge him by his clothes. A few months ago he was immaculate. What you see now is what being out of work has done to him. Look at what unemployment can do to a man, Auntie. No work, no house, no food. So listen, if you're not still waiting for that man, hire this one. Won't you consider it?"

"Certainly I can," said the old woman. "But would he accept my offer?"

"Hey! You. Open your eyes, brother. Look, this woman here is offering you work!"

Vasfi opened his eyes to look at the woman in amazement. "Are you talking to me?"

"Are you stupid or what? Who else would I be talking to, you dolt?" The woman in the green coat walked over to his bench.

"Look. You see that old lady over there? She's going to hire you. The storm did a lot of damage to her house and garden. You're going to do the repairs. I'm thinking this job will suit you well."

Vasfi turned to look at the old woman. She was small and delicate, and wearing a black silk headscarf which, though old, was perfectly clean and had been ironed with care. Seated on the bench, she looked almost like a young girl. She had her hands placed on her knees, and she was sitting up straight.

Though her face was covered in wrinkles, her large and remarkably young-looking eyes reminded Vasfi of his mother. Not only that, but the old woman was looking at him in surprise, as if she recognized him!

"Hey you," said the woman in the green coat. "Didn't you hear what I just told you. Come on now. Nod! Look, this nice lady offered you work, I say. If it suits your highness, you can accept."

Vasfi still didn't understand.

"Work, did you say? Who's offering me work?"

"Hey, lumber merchant! Wake up! How stupid can you be! I've been talking for an hour now, and the idiot's still playing games. Hey now. How many times do I have to tell you. This nice lady is offering you work. Would you like to work today?"

Vasfi jumped up, suddenly wide awake.

"Of course I'd be happy to work. That's all I've wanted—to work."

His heart was pounding.

"Do you see that, dear Auntie?" said the woman in the green coat. "Look at how happy he is." Turning to Vasfi, she burst out laughing. "Oh, what a lucky man you are. Don't you ever forget this blessing from God."

Then she fixed her collar and made for the door. As she left, she said, "Thank you so much, dear Auntie. I thank you so very much. You've done me a very great kindness. But I'd better leave now. If the stationmaster finds me here, he'll have me out on my ear."

With that, she left the waiting room.

Vasfi turned to the old woman, who was looking at him intently.

"I'm hoping that I'm not incapable of the jobs you need done," he murmured.

"No, my child. It's just that the storm blew off my garden fence and knocked down my trees. That's all I need help with."

"Very good, then. I shall do my best to repair the damage. I am very happy to take this on."

"In that case, let's go. My house is not far."

The old woman headed for the door. As Vasfi followed her, he felt peace in his heart. For the first time since he had taken his first trudging steps out of prison, there was a spring in his step.

After walking down a few narrow streets, they turned into a street that bordered onto the wall of an old palace. They came to a stop in front of a little two-story

163

house with iron bars on its windows. Icicles were swinging from the branches of the great tree in front. In the frozen light of the sun, they sparkled like crystal.

Walking through the gate, Vasfi's heart jumped. For the first time in twelve years, he was nearing a house. They entered an earthen courtyard. On the opposite side there were several steps as wide as the house itself, which led to a landing on which stood two doors. A clean white cloth on the first step served as a mat. On it a few pairs of slippers were carefully arranged. There was also a pair of clogs. Vasfi trembled at the sight of all this. For it reminded him of that immaculate little house where he'd spent his childhood and youth. How he longed for the Vasfi he'd been then. But that Vasfi was gone. How ashamed he felt to be entering this house in such filthy clothes. It wasn't right, he felt. He couldn't move. But it warmed his heart to hear this old woman addressing him in such a sweet voice. "Come, my child!" Especially since this sweet-voiced old woman's eyes looked so much like his mother's.

"My shoes are caked with mud," he murmured.

The old woman leaned down, picked up a pair of men's slippers and handed them to Vasfi. Then she took off her shoes and put on her own slippers.

After donning those comfortable slippers, he followed the old woman up the stairs. They entered one of the rooms. In front of the window was a sedir that went the full length of the room. It was covered in the same bright white calico as the curtains. There was a sheet-iron stove in the corner. A little brazier sat in front of it. All there was in this room was a table, a chest of drawers, and a few chairs.

With a smile, the old woman gestured toward the sedir.

"Please, my son. Sit down."

She took off her shawl. Now she was wearing only a white headscarf that fell to her shoulders. Picking up the brazier, she placed it in front of Vasfi. Then she sat down across from him and began to make coffee. Vasfi watched in wonder as her tiny, wrinkled hands went about their work. When the coffee was ready, she poured it from the pot into a tiny cup and passed it to Vasfi.

"May I offer you a cigarette?"

"Thank you."

The old woman said nothing while Vasfi drank his coffee, but her eyes never left him. When Vasfi was done, she said, "Let's get to work." She stood up.

"Yes . . ."

In no time, he was in the garden. It was a small garden, so like the one where he had played as a child and where on a summer's day he had first seen the girl for whom he'd sacrificed his life. The gardens of his childhood . . . In some parts of this garden there were drifts of snow that were even higher, whiter . . .

Sparrows were flitting through the air.

Vasfi set about chopping down the broken cherry branches and went about his work. How good it felt to use his muscles, which had been idle for so long.

At noon the old lady told him his food was ready and he could stop working. Vasfi expected to eat separately, but he saw a small table set for a meal for two. The old woman was treating him like a guest. Such gratitude he felt to sit down at this beautifully laid table, to partake of such food. So different from chomping on a heel of bread under the bridge, like an animal.

The woman was not the talkative sort. She said nothing of herself, nor did she ask Vasfi questions.

Vasfi worked until late to finish his jobs. Soon he would be leaving this clean house to return to homelessness.

Never again to know the joy of walking inside.

He thought of the cold, ruthless, merciless night awaiting him, and he shivered.

He went in to tell the old woman that his work was done.

"Thank you, my son. Come with me now. I've prepared you a hot bath, I thought you might like to get yourself clean. It brings peace, to get clean after this sort of work. You'll find clean underwear there, and a pair of trousers, and a jacket. A friend's son was going to help me with all this, so I prepared them for him. Now they're yours. You deserve them. You did the work."

All this brought a peace Vasfi would never forget. Clean underwear, hot water, soap . . .

When she saw him standing there, clean, with his hair combed, she smiled.

"Now we shall eat our supper."

"Supper? But I think I must be taking advantage of your kindness."

"No, dear. I've never liked eating alone. I am very glad I shall not have to do so this evening."

"But . . ."

"Is there anyone waiting for you?"

"No. I have no one in this world."

"Then stay here with me. It's hard to eat alone."

Thinking of the terrible solitude awaiting him, he said, "Yes, it's very hard to be alone."

So that night he ate supper with the old woman, and then he helped her with the dishes. He cleared the table. And then he said, "The time has come for me to take my leave."

Had the woman any idea how much he dreaded the fearful endless nights ahead?

Vasfi's shoulders were already shrinking at the prospect of the cold awaiting him. Who can say what the old women felt or understood. When Vasfi opened the door to let in a rush of icy air, she pushed the door shut and in a hoarse voice she murmured, "Don't go. Where are you going to go on a night as cold as this?" she pleaded. "I have a room upstairs, I can prepare a bed there for you."

Vasfi stopped short. Outside the wind continued to howl.

"All you've done for me . . . you've done so much . . . how could I ever accept such kindness?"

"Leave your empty words to one side. Shut the door. This is not kindness. It's very cold outside. That wind is as cold as ice. That room upstairs has been empty for a long time."

The woman turned her head to keep him from seeing the compassion in her eyes. Slowly Vasfi closed the door. He stayed in the room. It hadn't warmed up yet. He shivered under the thick quilt.

His heart was pounding, so much so that he struggled to breathe, because this lavender-scented bed with its clean sheets reminded him of his old house, his youth, and his beloved mother.

Suddenly Vasfi thought of happiness, and again this word reminded him of the woman with the black beret. Where was she now, he wondered. What was she doing? As she wandered these snowy icy streets tonight, could she still think of happiness? What a terrible night this would be for those still wandering to find a place to take shelter.

Suddenly Vasfi felt less content in his pristine bed. For he was thinking of all those outside with nowhere to go. Especially that poor, wan, fragile little woman; that lost creature wandering homeless in the streets of this great city . . .

There was no question in his mind how eternally grateful he was, to have found refuge with the old woman, even if it was for only one night. But suddenly the peace and happiness this night had brought him was no longer. Because happiness could not come from compassion. This good-hearted old woman could not change the way things were. Compassion lacked the power to change the terrifying reality of the streets. Where there was no comfort or peace, there could be no happiness either.

WHEN HE awoke the next morning in his clean warm sheets, he felt a great fear. Was he now to return to his vagrant life?

When he left the house, the old woman gave him a coat as a gift. Even so, he felt colder than usual. He was shivering. As he left, he said, "I don't know how I can ever thank you for your kindness. How can I ever make it up to you?"

"That is easy, my son. If I brought you any happiness, that makes me happy, too. I'm an old woman who has been left alone. You can come to visit me now and then. For now, we are even."

He was in no doubt that her words were sincere. For this reason he wished to visit her as soon as he could. But he lacked the courage to visit her as a vagrant beggar.

He wished he didn't have to leave the house of this woman who had so quickly made a new man of him. He loved that house. He even needed it. During his time in that little house, he had not felt dead.

HE SPENT two nights at a small hotel. He only left it to go past the Kadıköy ferry station a few times. Why was he going there? Perhaps it was to see the woman with the black beret. He didn't even know this, but every time he

169

went, he looked for her everywhere, and it troubled him greatly not to find her.

Lacking the money to pay for a third night, he was obliged to leave the hotel. He took refuge in one of his hated coffeehouses. "I don't want to live like this anymore," he said. "No going back to the way things were." He kept his eyes open, watching the door. He couldn't sleep.

At six in the morning he left the coffeehouse and headed down Yüksekkaldırım toward Karaköy. Passing a row of little shops he stopped suddenly. Perhaps one of their owners might have a job for him to do? Sweep the floor, for example, or wash the windows . . .

The first refusal did not discourage him. "I have to make a bit of money," he thought. As he walked down the hill, he kept going into shops and asking for work. He walked into the third shop. "I'm out of work," he said. "I want to earn a few kurush. I was wondering if you might have a job for me?"

This man had a few rubbish bins that needed emptying. The fifth had two baskets that needed carrying. He did these jobs with enthusiasm.

A week later, he knocked on the door of the little red house. He was holding a modest present he'd bought for his elderly friend. She was delighted with it. As they sat together on either side of the brazier, a wave of peace and happiness passed through Vasfi. Gazing at her wrinkled face, he forgot the grueling week he'd been through. Those sad days of going from door to door seeking work . . .

Sitting there under that warm and welcoming roof gave him courage. He wanted to show this woman who had done him such kindness that he had decided to lift himself up from the hole he'd fallen into.

How happy he felt next to this old woman who, be it from compassion or the goodness in her heart, had found the courage to take a wretched stranger into her house. Perhaps never even thinking of the possible dangers, she had treated him like a guest, and found herself unwilling to send him back into the streets and the icy wind.

VASFI WAS very happy in the company of this good woman.

What he felt for her was much more than gratitude. He was deeply in awe of her. Because now they were seeing each other more often. There was between them a bond of compassion. When Vasfi looked at the old woman, he thought of his mother. The same compassion in her eyes, the same sweetness. She busied herself around him, never asking him a thing about his life. They just talked about this and that together, as if they'd known each other forever.

EVERY MORNING Vasfi went out to look for work, returning to the house in the evening. The woman insisted that he move in with her.

"I'll give you my son's room."

"How is that? You have a son?"

"I had a son. A beautiful son who looked so very much like you . . ."

"The day I find work, I shall gratefully move into your son's room." Then, in a lower voice, he added, "My mother was beautiful like you. A good woman, like you."

One morning, while he was sweeping in front of a little shop, he felt a hand on his shoulder. Turning his head, he was astonished to see Sami, one of his friends from prison.

"Sami!"

"Yes, it's Sami! So we got through it, didn't we? I'm so glad to see you. It looks like you've landed on your feet."

"If you say so. But I still haven't found a job. It's six months now since I got out."

"You're right. It's not easy. Listen, maybe I can find you a way out." With a smile, he continued, "I'm working in construction now. The boss is a childhood friend. If this weren't the case, I'd still be out of work like you. I know they need someone in the office. Here's the address. Come before four and I'll be there. Okay?"

"Of course. I'll be there."

He shook Sami's hand.

"Thank you," he said. His heart overflowing with gratitude.

———

THAT AFTERNOON Vasfi went to the office where Sami was waiting for him. By the time he got back to Karaköy, night had fallen. The gladness he felt inside him was very much like happiness. Once again his mind turned to one of his worst days, and the woman in the black beret. As she walked the streets in misery, did she still believe in happiness?

He decided to stop off at Kadıköy ferry station before heading back to the little red house to tell his old friend the good news. He was hoping to find the woman in the black beret sitting there. And there she was, in her usual corner. Vasfi had never seen her looking as tired as she looked today. It was clear she had given up the fight now. She looked bewildered. Vasfi went over to her.

"Hello . . ."

The woman looked up at him, surprised. It was clear she didn't recognize him at first. And then, she said, "So it's you?"

"How are you? Are you well?"

The woman shrugged lightly. It was clear from her face that she wasn't well at all. Vasfi's heart went out to this woman, who was still beautiful, even in her wretched state. What he felt was something close to compassion.

"I'd like to do something for you," he said.

The young woman tried to smile. "Thank you very much," she said. Her sadness was so great that Vasfi lacked the courage to say another thing. In silence he sat down beside her. When the woman stood up a moment later, he stood up, too.

The young woman was swaying as she walked. Vasfi wanted to hold her by the arm, but he didn't dare. For a time they walked together in silence. When they reached Dolmabahçe Palace, the woman suddenly stopped.

It was pitch-dark. You couldn't see the sea, but you could hear it. You could smell the moss in the air and taste salt on your lips. From time to time, a wave splashed onto the shore. A wild wind cracked its whip. Behind them were the sparkling lights of one of Istanbul's wealthy neighborhoods. Before them the invisible wind and the moaning waves and, here and there, a light on the Anatolian shore. For a time they stood side by side without speaking.

Then in a tired voice the young woman said, "I'm cold."

It was true. Her whole body was shaking. He took off his coat and put it around her shoulders. Placing his hands on her shoulders, he asked, "Are you sure you aren't ill?"

"No, I'm not ill. I'm hungry."

Her answer was as calm as it was terrible. Now the woman began to sob. Vasfi did not hesitate to wrap his arms around her. There they stayed. Slowly the woman's tears abated. Then they stopped. The waves were louder now. The wind fiercer.

"It's wrong to lose hope," he murmured. "Everything can change. I forgot to tell you. I found work."

"What—you found work?"

"Yes, I did. I found work. That's not everything, but it's still pretty wonderful!"

Then he took the young woman by the hand. "So let's go, my girl! Our first task is to find you a room. Then we'll go and get ourselves something to eat."

They looked at each other for a long time. Then, as the wind howled around them, they walked hand in hand back into the city.

ABOUT THE AUTHOR

Suat Derviş (Istanbul, 1905–1972) is one of the leading female authors of Turkish literature. She was educated in Germany, where she wrote articles for newspapers and journals. After the rise of fascism, she returned to Turkey in 1932. She became renowned for her novels, which were serialized in Turkish newspapers and often centered around the tragic lives of lost, lonely, and struggling people in urban Turkey. In 1941 she began publishing *Yeni Edebiyat* ("New Literature"), a biweekly magazine on art and literature. A dedicated socialist, she was placed under house arrest for a short period of time following the publication of her book *Why Do I Admire Soviet Russia*. After her release, and a change of government in Turkey, she voluntarily exiled herself from 1953 to 1963. With the publication of *The Prisoner of Ankara* in 1957, she became the first female Turkish author to publish a novel in Europe. The novel received critical acclaim from *Le Monde* and the literary periodical *Les Lettres Françaises,* and was published in Turkish eleven years later. Her novel *In the Shadow of the Yalı* was published by Other Press in 2021.

ABOUT THE TRANSLATOR

Maureen Freely is the author of seven novels, and a former journalist who focused on literature, social justice, and human rights. Well known as a translator of Nobel Laureate Orhan Pamuk, she has brought into English several Turkish classics as well as newer work by Turkey's rising stars. As chair of the Translator's Association and more recently as president and chair of English PEN, she has campaigned for writers and freedom of expression internationally. She teaches at the University of Warwick.